SECRET OF LIGHT

For Peter,
swordsman,
construction expert,
and appreciative listener.

SECRET OF LIGHT

kc dyer

A BOARDWALK BOOK
A MEMBER OF THE DUNDURN GROUP
TORONTO

Editor: Barry Jowett
Copy-Editor: Jennifer Bergeron
Design: Jennifer Scott
Printer: Transcontinental

National Library of Canada Cataloguing in Publication Data

Dyer, K. C.
  Secret of light / K.C. Dyer.

ISBN 1-55002-477-9

I. Title.

PS8557.Y474S38 2003   jC813'.6   C2003-904049-6

1   2   3   4   5   07   06   05   04   03

Canada

THE CANADA COUNCIL | LE CONSEIL DES ARTS
FOR THE ARTS | DU CANADA
SINCE 1957 | DEPUIS 1957

ONTARIO ARTS COUNCIL
CONSEIL DES ARTS DE L'ONTARIO

We acknowledge the support of the **Canada Council for the Arts** and the **Ontario Arts Council** for our publishing program. We also acknowledge the financial support of the **Government of Canada** through the **Book Publishing Industry Development Program** and **The Association for the Export of Canadian Books**, and the **Government of Ontario** through the **Ontario Book Publishers Tax Credit** program, and the **Ontario Media Development Corporation's Ontario Book Initiative.**

Printed and bound in Canada.
Printed on recycled paper.

www.dundurn.com

Dundurn Press
8 Market Street
Suite 200
Toronto, Ontario, Canada
M5E 1M6

Dundurn Press
2250 Military Road
Tonawanda NY
U.S.A. 14150

Acknowledgements

I humbly offer my most grateful and heartfelt thanks to all the people who have held my hand, literally, figuratively, and electronically, as I have stumbled down the road toward the writing of this book. On this journey to my wildest dreams, I could ask for no greater company.

Thanks to …

… my friends and family for enthusiasm, emotional sustenance, and a total willingness to engage in lengthy discussions about what they are reading this week. Special thanks to the leaders of my Lions Bay and Calgary cheering sections: Linda, Ingrid, Sue, Kelly, Meaghan, Audrey, and Lisa.

… my gracious and generous editor Barry Jowett, and also to the keen-eyed Jennifer Bergeron and Andrea Pruss.

… Jennifer Scott for yet again weaving her magic to create the consummate cover.

… Kirk Howard for his support and encouragement.

… *la mia amica Federica Padovani, per la sua assistenza in tradurre la mia storia, ogni sbagli che io ho fatto sono solamante miei. Grazie.*

… the members of the Compuserve Writers' Forum for the on-line camaraderie and seemingly unending source of invaluable arcana.

… my writing compatriots: Marsha Forchuk Skrypuch, Pamela Capriotti Martin, Kate Coombs, Linda Gerber, Julie Kentner, Bernice Lever, Moira Thompson, and the other denizens of the North Shore Writers' Association and KidCrit for their sharp eyes, unflagging support, and good humour.

… the incomparable Diana Gabaldon for her kind words, deeds, and inspiration.

… my readers, with whom I share a priceless bond: the love of a good story.

September brings school and best friends return,
But an enemy, too, shows his face.
A fresh goal for the term means a Fair and hard work,
Classes new, yet an odd sense of place.

To remember old times, a trip through a cave,
No glyphs but a sketch, bright and true.
Ancient light cannot shine, yet it summons and calls,
A wind rises, the past beckons anew.

Among Renaissance lands, a new day is drawn,
Rebirth in the Arts, all rejoice.
Possibility raised; a prediction unheard,
A hasty retreat not by choice.

Thrust out of time, a return must be made,
Obsessions squeeze tight as a fist.
A seeker is lost, a couple is joined,
A dog disappears in the mist.

A soldier, an artist, a sculptor, a friend,
Can one man hold the key to all time?
Traveller as thief; is the prize all it seems?
Does an enemy witness the crime?

Study intense, friends ignored, school work shunned,
Yet the answer remains beyond reach.
Long dark night of despair, in the end all that's gleaned,
Is a lesson just friendship can teach.

A Renaissance Fair marks the end of a year;
But words from a wise woman warn.
An unwelcome traveller, a poignant goodbye,
Old worries anew must be borne.

Kidnap, frantic search, and a dash through the dark,
A dome and a monk and a clock.
A final betrayal, a fire explodes,
Inferno consumes all but rock.

The beacon is ash, route through time seared away,
Hope for peace, winter break is in sight.
Yet reflection brings pain, for how high was the cost
To unravel the Secret of Light?

CHAPTER ONE

Darrell sat propped, comfortable against warm rocks. Leaning her head against a boulder, she gazed at the fine, blue sea with eyes closed to a slit against the setting sun. Delaney stirred under her hand and nestled into a more comfortable spot on the sand. He lay at her side, head on his paws, eyes watchful.

From this angle, Darrell could turn her head and just see one corner of Eagle Glen School's north tower. Constructed of grey granite, the tower looked as though it were standing guard over the rugged coastline. She craned her neck to see more of the tower, her mind filled with speculation. A whole school year here at Eagle Glen! There was a lot she wanted to learn, and not much of it was academic.

Delaney raised his head and Darrell shifted her focus. Two figures emerged from the winding path leading down from the cliffs. One of the figures waved and they began to run. Darrell's heart lifted. "Good spotting, Delaney," she said, and ruffled the dog's fur. "It's about time those two got here."

Darrell glanced down at the sketchbook in her lap. The wind rippled the pages, and a few grains of sand skittered through to settle in the binding. Each page held a sketch or a drawing depicting a young girl with brown hair engaged in various activities: swimming, running, riding a bike. The girl in the sketches differed from the artist who drew them by only a single element. She had two sound legs.

In seconds, a girl with short, red hair standing up in spikes off her freckled forehead collapsed breathless on the sand. Puffing behind her, a tall boy with almond eyes was carrying a heavy backpack.

"You only won because I was lugging this," he said, grinning.

"Ha!" The girl struggled to speak, still panting heavily. "It's just my — superior physical — conditioning."

Darrell laughed, her melancholy mood forgotten. "I'm glad to see you guys. You need to take it easy on Brodie, Kate. He's not as young as he used to be."

Brodie Sun nodded. "Yup. My birthday was last week. Got a whole set of new tap hammers for fossils."

Kate Clancy rolled her eyes. "More stuff to weigh down your backpack."

Darrell beamed at her friends, now settled in comfort on the sand. "What've you got there, Brodie? Some of your birthday presents?"

Brodie flashed a guilty grin. "Oh, you know, just some stuff..."

"Stuff for looking at cave walls, maybe?" interjected Kate.

"Maybe. It's getting a bit late today, though. And we've got our orientation session tonight…" His voice trailed off, the longing in it palpable.

Kate laughed. "Brodie, you are so predictable. Once a fossil geek, always a fossil geek."

Brodie pulled the pack across the sand, leaving a deep track. "You're just mad you don't have your laptop with you," he teased. "Or have you given up computer programming in the past month?"

Kate raised an eyebrow. "Actually, you guys will be proud of me. I spent the last two weeks at the studio near my house, practising tae kwon do. I'm going to try for my fourth-degree black belt when I go home for the holidays."

"Man!" Brodie shook his head in mock consternation. "Two weeks away from your computer? You must have been in agony."

Delaney rolled over and set his paw on Brodie's hand.

"How you doin', Delaney boy?" Brodie ruffled the dog's fur and scratched behind his ears. "Look at this guy, Kate. He doesn't look too much like a stray anymore."

Kate smiled and buried her face in the dog's ruff. "Nope. Looks like he's been living the good life lately." She ran her hand along his side. "I can hardly feel his ribs, Darrell. What've you been feeding this boy?"

Darrell leaned forward indignantly. "He is *not* fat. He's just happy to have a real home now, that's all!"

Kate laughed and punched Brodie's backpack into an uncomfortable-looking pillow. "Yeah. I guess his log house is gone for good." She lay down and gazed across the sand to the spot where the hollow log had once rested on the beach. "Must've been quite a storm to pull that giant old tree out to sea."

"He doesn't need it anymore, anyway. Professor Tooth gave me permission to keep him in my room."

Kate followed Darrell's glance toward the school. "Feels good to be back, eh?"

Darrell nodded. "I can't believe it. We get to spend a whole year here instead of going back to the stupid school in the city."

Kate pulled a water bottle out of Brodie's pack and grinned at him as she stole a sip. "Aw, c'mon Darrell. That school wasn't so bad. You just had some rough days there."

Darrell's smile faded. "It was a terrible place."

"Well, no school can compare to Eagle Glen," Brodie interrupted. "I've never had a summer like this one before..."

"And probably never will again," interjected Kate, seeming to catch Darrell's mood. "The glyphs on the cave wall are all gone, Brodie. Eagle Glen will be just like every other school now. I bet — Hey!"

A shower of rocks cascaded over the cliff, setting off tiny explosions of shards and sand. Kate and Brodie scrambled out of the way of the dusty fallout and Darrell jumped up. A large chunk narrowly missed the spot where Delaney had been lying and rolled against the rock face with a hollow *thunk*. Looking up, they could see a distant figure stride away from the cliff's edge in the direction of the school. Delaney growled low in his throat, his hackles high.

"I don't know," said Brodie, brushing a fine layer of dust off his pants. "Somehow I don't think Eagle Glen has revealed all its surprises just yet." He stood and hoisted his pack onto one shoulder. "Let's go see who would want to send us such a warm welcome. We can have a look through the cave later."

The sun slipped under the horizon and the warmth slid out of the day like a hand into cool water. The damp air caused an ache to rise in Darrell's right leg, and she limped a little as she found her footing on the rocky shore. They gathered their things and, Delaney in the lead, trekked back along the beach toward the school.

Darrell climbed the winding path with her characteristic hop-skip step, following Delaney on the well-worn trail. The discomfort she'd been feeling bloomed into pain shooting up her right leg, but she tightened her lips and increased her pace. In the three long years since she'd lost part of her leg and her father in one terrible night, she had hardened herself to letting anyone share the ache she felt in her heart or in her leg. Brodie and Kate had helped, and she was not going to let a little ache slow her down.

The cool air of the early fall twilight lifted the hair on Darrell's arms, and the sudden breeze stirring the leaves of the old arbutus in the school garden made her shiver. Students milled around the front of the school, and she watched Kate frown at the sight of the new faces.

"Well, this is a pain. Look at all these strangers taking over our school. I wonder which one threw those rocks?"

Darrell looked over the crowd. "I wonder, too. Maybe it was an accident."

Brodie shrugged. "Probably." He glanced at Kate. "You're funny, Kate. It's only been our school for a couple of months. You sound kind of possessive."

"I feel possessive, too," interrupted Darrell. She patted Kate's shoulder. "This is the only school I have ever liked. I've made friends here for the first time in a long time," she added quietly.

Kate snorted. "Some friends — one computer techie and one fossil geek."

Darrell grinned. "Well, you two are the lucky ones, I guess. You get to be friends with an *artiste*." She pushed Brodie's backpack so he staggered into Kate. "You'd better get rid of that thing before orientation," she said, looking at her watch. "I'm going to take a quick run through to the art studio. I'll meet you guys in the dining hall in ten minutes."

"Yeah, I've got to go get my stuff," said Kate, neatly sidestepping Brodie's giant pack. "I'll grab my laptop and save us all seats."

"See ya in ten!" Brodie resettled his heavy pack on his shoulders and began the long climb up the old stairs to the boys' rooms on the third floor.

Darrell smiled at her easel, feeling in a way like she was greeting an old friend. She glanced around the art room. Everything was, of course, just as it had been when she left a scant three weeks before, yet she felt a rush of emotion that the room was still here, ready to wrap her in its warm embrace. The place even smelled like home. She couldn't wait to begin.

"I've got ten minutes, I don't have to wait," she said aloud, and then jumped at the sound of her own voice echoing off the curved glass windows of the large room. She laughed at her own reaction, but still looked around to make sure no one had overheard her talking to herself. A quick glance confirmed she was indeed alone, and, safe from prying ears, she continued the conversation.

"What I need is some paint," she began, as she strode over to an open cupboard door and started to rummage. "Some paint and some lovely, thick Arches paper and my new brushes." Arms full of supplies, Darrell dashed over to her station and began to fill the small, wheeled trolley standing beside the draped easel. From her backpack on the floor she pulled a soft cotton towel rolled and tied with string. Laying the roll on the tall tabletop near the easel, she carefully untied and then unrolled the cloth — a soft case loaded with paintbrushes.

Darrell pulled the drapery off her easel and gasped. Instead of a blank canvas, propped under the oilcloth drape was the picture she had painted last summer. All the manic energy drained out of her as she stared, mesmerized, into the streets of Mallaig, a small fishing village on the west coast of Scotland, as they had been six hundred years before.

"I took the liberty of having it framed."

Darrell's head snapped up and she found herself gazing into the deep green eyes of the school principal, Professor Myrtle Tooth, standing beside the art room door.

Darrell's voice caught in her throat. "I — I can see you have," she said, at last. "Thank you."

"Consider it a welcome back gift," the principal said, smiling. She stepped away from the easel and spoke in her familiar measured tone. "I want you to know someone else honours your work as much as you do." She paused. "It is a beautiful piece. Very dark and mysterious — rife with speculation."

"What do you mean?" asked Darrell.

Professor Tooth smiled and looked at her watch. "A beautifully executed painting is like an interesting person — multi-layered. What can be seen on the surface is not always an indicator of what lies beneath." Darrell was about to reply when the door to the studio flung open and Kate surged in, narrowly avoiding the principal. She screeched to a halt beside Darrell's easel and smiled a guilty apology.

"Professor Tooth! I was looking for Darrell. It's almost time for orientation."

The principal nodded and glanced again at her watch. "I see. Thank you, Kate, for helping me keep to my schedule."

She turned to Darrell. "I hope you are happy with the frame. Perhaps, with your permission, we may display this work in the front office? I'm sure Mrs. Follett could do with a change from the dreadful Monet print she has hanging there now."

Darrell nodded and watched the door close behind Professor Tooth. Kate slapped her hand on a table. "Great! First day back and I practically crash into the principal." She gazed at Darrell, speculation in her eyes. "What was all that about, anyway? Did I interrupt something?"

Darrell shook her head and replaced the cover on the easel. "You know, it's kinda strange," she said, as she slid her tray of supplies back into place, "but every conversation I have with that woman leaves me feeling she knows way more about me than I do myself."

Kate shrugged and held open the door. "Let's go to orientation. Brodie's there saving our seats. And maybe Professor Tooth will give us a few answers, for a change!"

The dining hall echoed with the sounds and movements of milling bodies. Unlike most gatherings populated by large groups of teens, a feeling of uncertainty tinged the atmosphere like smoke through a firehouse. Darrell looked around, interested in the pervasive feeling. Eagle Glen was a new school for most of the kids here, though she knew some had switched from the European campus. Uncharted territory. Everyone she could see rustling their papers and scraping their chairs seemed touched by first-day-at-a-new-school nerves.

Darrell smiled. Her summertime experiences had given her a taste of Eagle Glen, though she felt like she had more questions about the school and its principal than ever. *Guess we'll learn soon enough.*

Darrell and Kate stepped across a tangle of legs to slide into seats beside Brodie. Kate dug through her bag. "I think I forgot my timetable in the room," she whispered.

Brodie leaned around Darrell. "What? You mean you haven't programmed it into your laptop already? How lax of you." He chuckled gently.

Kate smirked and pulled out her laptop. "Why, thank you for reminding me, Brodie," she said with satisfaction. "As a matter of fact, I have done just that."

Brodie groaned. "Unbelievable," he muttered.

"Shhh," hissed Darrell. "Here comes Professor Tooth."

The principal stepped onto a raised platform and looked out at the sea of faces. The tables had been pushed back against the walls and windows, and the open space was filled with chairs. Without raising her hand or even an eyebrow, quiet dropped like a blanket over the room. She smiled.

"I'm not sure what to make of a silence like this one. However, based on my years of experience as a teacher, I realize I should enjoy these moments when I can find them." She stepped forward and her eyes seemed to take in every face. "I must say I am filled with a tremendous sense of excitement this evening. As many of you know, this is the second fully functioning campus of Eagle Glen School. The first has been running successfully in Europe for more than a decade. I know you must all be eager to have the new year underway and hear more about your classes, so I will keep my remarks very brief."

A murmur ran through the group, and Darrell settled herself more comfortably. If this speech was like any of those she had listened to from previous principals, it would probably go on a lot longer than everyone would like. Still — she looked around at the faces of the other students. It was weird, but everyone seemed to be paying attention.

"Eagle Glen is a unique school. We view each student's education very seriously here, and recognize that much learning in the life of a teenager comes from more than the pages of a textbook. Eagle Glen is a school where you will follow the customary path to higher learning — with a twist. Each student is encouraged — expected — to find the path best suited to him or her. Some of you may find," and here Darrell could have sworn Professor Tooth's eyes twinkled directly at her, "the path is far more interesting and involved than you might ever have expected."

Darrell felt Kate's elbow dig into her side, and she pressed her own knuckles hard against the smile she felt threatening to turn into a laugh.

"You will now be assembled according to form, and each group of students will go through timetables with its form teacher. Each form teacher will be available during school hours to answer any questions you may have. After school hours, this job passes to the head students. Elections for these positions will be held next week. Until then, your form teacher will give you all the information you need. Would the fourth form please stand? I'll ask you to follow Mr. Neuron to the math centre."

There was a general rustling and muttering as a ragged group of students gathered their things and filed out of the room. Darrell was stunned. The speech had been less than a minute long. Professor Tooth had been true to her word.

Kate whispered in Darrell's ear, a note of panic in her voice. "What about Brodie? If classes are divided by age, he'll be a year ahead of us!"

Darrell felt a pang of worry, and turned to Brodie, her eyes wide. "Are you in first form or second?" she demanded in a loud whisper.

"Second." But Brodie was grinning. "Don't worry, I've talked to Professor Tooth. It'll all work out, you'll see."

Puzzled, Darrell looked up to see Professor Tooth had gathered the third form and sent them off with a female teacher she didn't recognize. Glancing around the room, Darrell could see there were fewer than thirty students left.

"Second form? Please follow Mr. Dickerman to the rock lab."

Professor Tooth had begun summoning the final group when a door banged open at the back of the room. Darrell was craning her neck, looking for the source of the disruption, when she felt a hand grip her upper arm and squeeze.

"Ow!" She looked down to see her arm caught in Kate's iron-tight grip. Darrell opened her mouth to complain, but closed it when she saw Kate's expression. The colour had drained out of her friend's face and her freckles stood out like spots of rust on the pale skin.

Darrell followed Kate's gaze to the door and her stomach dropped into her shoes. Leaning on the doorframe, a smirk on his face, was Conrad Kennedy.

Professor Tooth's voice was brisk. "Mr. Kennedy. I'm afraid you are a trifle late, but if you will wait a moment, I will see you to your teacher. Would the first form please follow Mr. Gill to the library?"

Darrell's heart hammered in her chest.

Kate turned and met Darrell's gaze. "What's he doing here?" she squeaked.

"I don't know." Darrell's voice choked as she rubbed the vivid red marks Kate's fingers had left on her arm. "I guess we're about to find out."

Chapter Two

Darrell dragged a heavy, stuffed chair over the uneven planks of the library floor to a spot beside Kate. Fifteen kids were gathered in the group, almost equally divided between girls and boys. Flopping into the chair, she rubbed her right knee and gazed around at the new faces. She leaned forward and adjusted the prosthesis under her jeans. A low ache still throbbed in her leg, and she looked out one of the leaded glass windows of the library. The night was so black, all she could see was the reflection of the brightly lit room on the glass. The lashing of rain against the window confirmed what the ache in her leg had already told her.

"Sore leg?" Kate spoke in a low voice, and Darrell shook her head at her friend's concerned face.

"Oh, nothing to worry about — just the usual for a rainy night." She looked around and dropped her voice to a whisper. "Can you see Conrad anywhere?"

Kate peered over the back of her large wing chair. "Nope, not a sign of him. I can't believe it was really him! What d'you think he's doing here? I thought he was supposed to be in some kind of reform school in Ontario."

Darrell shrugged and was about to reply when Mr. Gill cleared his throat at the front of the room. Kate ripped a sheet out of her binder and passed it to Darrell. *Let's talk later*, it read.

Darrell nodded and turned to listen as Mr. Gill began to outline the calendar for the upcoming year.

Wind hurled rain against the windows, and Darrell snuggled deeper under her down quilt. She was warm and dry, it was midnight of her first night back at school, classes were scheduled to begin the following morning at eight-thirty, and she was as far from sleepy as it was possible to get. Fall had roared in with a vengeance, and the storm outside the windows perfectly reflected her state of mind, roiling with all the events of the day. Delaney lay curled in his creaky wicker bed on the floor.

"I look forward to getting to know all of you this year. Please don't hesitate to approach me at any time if you have questions or worries." The voice of Mr. Gill echoed in her head, and Darrell remembered how his eyes had lit up as he looked at her. *"It'll be great working with you again, Darrell."*

Yet his words twisted and swirled around the image of the smirking face at the back of the dining hall. Arthur Gill and Conrad Kennedy. Two more differing male figures she could not imagine, and yet they had both markedly changed her life this past summer. Conrad was a bully, a thief, a smuggler — and worse. She had last seen his sneering face as he was hauled off the beach by the RCMP in handcuffs.

That should have been the last of him. What's he doing here?

And Arthur Gill, the art teacher who had been her inspiration over the summer and was now the head teacher for the first form. He was a talented artist in his own right, and she had been so looking forward to working with him for a full school year. But would that change now that Conrad had appeared?

Darrell sat up, her crawling thoughts leaving her unable to get comfortable in any position. She snapped on the tiny book light she kept beside her bed and picked up her sketch pad and charcoal from her bedside table. In the glow from the small bulb she saw Delaney lift his head. He met her eyes and his tail thumped once, and with a few gentle creaks he settled back into his wicker bed, head on his paws.

"At least you can sleep," Darrell muttered, and then jumped at the sound of another voice.

"Maybe he can, but I can't." Kate's whisper carried from her bed across the room. "Too much to think about." She grabbed her quilt and scampered over to settle like a small nesting bird at the foot of Darrell's bed. Leaning back against the window, she gestured at a lump in the middle of the third bed in the room. Gentle snores emerged from the pile of covers. "Lily doesn't seem to be having any problem," she commented dryly.

Darrell grinned and glanced over at the third resident of the room. Lily Kyushu, who had shared a room with Darrell and Kate in the summer term, had quickly established a reputation for herself as a fast swimmer and a noisy sleeper. "Yeah, with Lily there, it feels like nothing's changed — and then I remember this summer and I feel like nothing will ever be the same again."

Kate nodded. "I know what you mean. So much happened in such a short time it's almost easier to pretend it didn't."

Darrell dropped her sketchbook into her lap and rubbed her forehead. "It's only our first day back and already things are not the way I expected."

"Yeah. We've got a new school year — and one seriously disturbed student."

"No kidding." Darrell fidgeted with the charcoal pencil, twisting it through her fingers with practiced ease. "I don't know how we're supposed to think about learning anything with that bully in the group."

"Well," said Kate sensibly, "we don't even know if he's in our class. I didn't see him after orientation, and there has to be some kind of mistake for him to be here in any case. Besides, if he *is* going to this school, he's sure to flunk out anyway." She ran her fingers through her short, red hair so it rose above her forehead in spikes. "Anyway, from the list that Mr. Gill gave us, it sounds like it's going to be a busy year."

"Yeah, I just hope some of it will be fun," Darrell answered absently, her mind on Conrad.

Kate rubbed her eyes. "I guess we'd better try to get some sleep," she said with a yawn. Wrapping her quilt around her shoulders, she slid off Darrell's bed and crawled back into her own. Her voice emerged, somewhat muffled, from under the covers. "Remind me to write my parents for some earplugs, would you? I forgot how loud Lily's nasal passages actually are."

"Um hmm." In spite of the noise from Lily's bed, after a few moments Darrell could hear Kate's breathing become slow and even. She tried to settle herself in her bed, but her brain wouldn't co-operate. She thought about the cave on the beach below the school and the glyphs that had pulled her back to the time of the Black Plague. Images of medieval Scotland swirled with thoughts of Conrad. It was a long time before her mind slowed down enough to allow sleep to claim her at last.

She was swimming through marshmallows and it wasn't easy. Her arms and legs felt like they were weighted with lead, and it was getting harder to breathe. Downright suffocating, in fact. Something had to be done. Darrell opened one eye.

"It's about time you entered the land of the living. You've missed breakfast entirely and you've only got ten minutes before class starts."

"What?" Darrell opened the other eye and glanced at her clock. She sat up and several pillows fell onto the floor.

"I *said* you'd better get moving. I must have fired ten pillows at your head before you woke up."

"Oh." Darrell yawned. "That explains the marsh-mallows." She reached down, batted a few pillows away, and grabbed her prosthesis from its place beside the bed.

"You've gotta get out of this habit of staying up so late. You'll never make your class."

Darrell raised an eyebrow. "Oh, and you were sleeping like a baby?"

Kate grinned and stuck a paper plate bearing a banana and a muffin onto Darrell's night table. "I brought you a mobile breakfast."

"Thanks." Darrell flew out the door to the bathroom, her arms filled with yesterday's clothes. Ten minutes later, she was sitting in Renaissance history class, swallowing the last bite of a dry carrot muffin.

"I need coffee," she whispered to Kate, who bulged her eyes at the door in response. Professor Tooth entered the room and the class fell into the amiable silence of a group ready to be entertained.

"As a prelude to today's lesson, I would like to invite all of you to a special meeting to be held in the dining hall this evening. Your form teacher may have mentioned something about the upcoming Renaissance fair, but full details will be available at the meeting. I bring this up not only to act as a reminder but to introduce the topic of the Renaissance fair, the subject of our lesson today."

Darrell felt a nudge against her left elbow and turned to see Kate sliding an open notebook under her arm.

RENAISSANCE FAIR!! was written in capital letters and underlined twice.

Darrell scribbled a reply and slid the notebook back. _So what?_

Kate smirked and scribbled *Dunk tank.* The next word was circled. *Lily.*

Darrell jotted a reply and pushed the notebook back. *Snore revenge?*

Kate's smile broadened and she nodded before turning her full attention to Professor Tooth. Darrell settled more comfortably in her seat and was soon drawn in by the teacher's words. She spent the rest of the class translating Professor Tooth's lesson into an elaborate sketch in her notebook, complete with festive tents, wandering minstrels, and a thieving pickpocket relieving a noble of his gold.

Class time flew by and before she knew it, Darrell was gathering her things and heading for the door.

"Ms. Connor, could you stay behind a moment, please? I'd like a word with you."

Darrell glanced up to see Professor Tooth standing by the door and closed her notebook guiltily. Maybe sketching wasn't one of Professor Tooth's approved notetaking methods.

The teacher smiled, and her green eyes gazed steadily into Darrell's. "I hope you enjoyed the lesson this morning. I meant it to serve as an apt introduction to one of the most magical eras of history."

Darrell breathed a silent sigh of relief. She clutched her notebook to her chest. "I can't wait until we get to study the artists. Mr. Gill told me we can spend some time learning the techniques Michelangelo used to paint the ceiling of the Sistine Chapel."

"Yes, I understand the subject is on Mr. Gill's agenda for this fall. However, I have something else I'd like to discuss with you for the moment. We have a new student I would like to introduce, though I do believe you have met before. Let's walk down to my office, shall we?"

Darrell was curious as she followed Professor Tooth down the hall to the office. Someone she had already met? Could it be one of the kids from her old school? She had grown to feel very protective of Eagle Glen, and she didn't feel it was the right school for many of the kids who had been so distant and rude to her at her old school in Vancouver. Staring at the floor and thinking these dark thoughts, she followed Professor Tooth and automatically turned to close the door.

When she turned back, the sight of the student standing by the window in the principal's office froze her to the spot in shock. How could she have been so stupid? Of course.

"When I saw you at orientation I thought there had been some kind of mistake," she gasped, looking at the pale, sulking face of Conrad Kennedy.

"You wish!" he snarled, then added, "You and me both, actually."

"There is no mistake." Professor Tooth's calm voice overrode Conrad's snarl. "Conrad has taken his place as a student at Eagle Glen as of today."

Darrell whirled to face the principal. "But what about everything that happened over the summer? I thought both he and his dad were going to jail!"

The principal looked serious. "The events of the summer are in the past, Darrell. Conrad's father has been incarcerated and Conrad was to be sent to a special school in Ontario."

Darrell felt her face flush and she glanced at Conrad's closed and sneering expression.

Professor Tooth spoke again. "It is my opinion Conrad will learn far more here than at a school for incorrigible children."

She turned to him. "I presume you are settled into your room?" When he nodded, she stepped forward and opened the door. "Then you just have time for lunch before your music class begins."

Conrad's face twisted into a grimace, and in three strides he reached the door. He leaned over and put his mouth beside Darrell's ear.

"Nice to see you again, Gimpy," he whispered, and slipped out of the office.

Darrell closed her eyes for a moment so her tears of anger and frustration wouldn't show. She struggled to find words — any words — that could possibly tell Professor Tooth how wrong she was to accept Conrad as a student at Eagle Glen. When she opened her mouth to protest, the teacher raised her hand.

"I am asking you to try not to judge this situation, Darrell. Conrad will be closely monitored here at Eagle Glen."

Professor Myrtle Tooth stepped over to her desk and sat down. Her clear, green eyes bored into Darrell's. "I know you have experienced some prejudice in your own life, Darrell. I'm not asking you to be friends with Conrad. All I'm asking is that you not actively sabotage the process."

Darrell nodded, not trusting herself to speak. How could Professor Tooth bring Conrad into the school?

Didn't the risk he posed outweigh any so-called benefit to him? Her mind spinning, she somehow found herself walking toward the art studio, clutching her notebook in white-knuckled hands.

Even after two hours with a paintbrush in her hand, Darrell had no trouble recognizing the feeling in her stomach as she walked to the dining room. Fear. Her mind still reeled with questions. What was he doing here? Why would Professor Tooth let such an awful person into the school? And what was Eagle Glen going to be like with Conrad as a new student?

Darrell looked around the dining room and spied Kate sitting with Brodie and Lily and a boy she didn't recognize at a table in the corner. She dropped her backpack at the door and headed to the lineup to choose her lunch. Her stomach twisted at the thought of eating anything, but she might as well go through the motions.

Darrell cast a critical eye across the choices for the day and selected lasagne, a dish reminiscent of one of her Uncle Frank's specialties. As she waited for a drink, she felt the tension begin to seep away. The dining hall was filled with students, all chattering and laughing. She was safe. The smell of the lasagne was rich and tomato-y and she was surprised to feel her stomach rumble in spite of her anxiety. She took her food and slid into a seat beside Kate, who was engaged in a heated discussion with the new boy at the table.

"It's just not right. He's a criminal, even if he was led astray by his father. He belongs in jail, not at the school closest to his dad's smuggling operation."

"I guess I missed a lot of excitement last summer," said the boy with a wry grin. "All I know is I heard the guy play guitar this morning and he's not bad. He seemed in a lousy mood at the beginning of the class, but by the end, everyone had put down their instruments to listen to him play."

"Conrad plays guitar?" Lily set her glass down so firmly she spilled her milk. "I can't believe that guy can do anything but get into trouble."

Darrell began to eat her lunch and glanced at Brodie. He smiled and looked pointedly at her arms. Darrell's hands were clean but paint began at her wrists and continued vividly past her elbows.

"Tough morning painting?" he asked. Darrell's mouth was full so she shook her head and rolled her eyes at him.

"Translation: 'Yeah, Brodie, isn't it obvious? I've been painting my fingers to the bone and I haven't eaten in days.'" He laughed at her expression.

Darrell swallowed and took a sip of water on which she promptly choked. Kate pounded her on the back.

"Nice first impression you're making with the new guy." She grinned.

Darrell wiped her streaming eyes on a napkin and managed to stop spluttering.

"I was painting all morning, and er — I didn't quite find the time for a shower before lunch." She coughed again.

"Once you get a hold of yourself, Darrell, I'll introduce you," Lily said brightly. Darrell frowned.

"I'm perfectly capable of introducing myself," she said, and looked across the table. "My name's Darrell Connor. I mostly work in the art program, as you can see." She glanced ruefully at her paint-speckled arms.

"I'm Paris Mercer. I saw you in history this morning, though I guess you didn't see me."

Darrell looked puzzled. "You're in our history class with Professor Tooth?"

Paris nodded. "My main interest is music, but I thought I'd give history a try." He paused for a moment and looked out the window of the dining room. The rain of the evening before was a distant memory, and late September sunshine dappled the waves. He turned back to the others. "This is an amazing place. I've only lived in the city and I didn't know it could be so beautiful out here. I figured it would be totally boring with nothing to do."

Darrell exchanged a meaningful glance with Brodie and Kate. "I wouldn't ever use the word *boring* to describe life at Eagle Glen," she said quietly. She gazed at Paris. "Sorry I don't remember you from history. With a name like Paris and blue hair, you don't exactly blend into the background!"

Brodie looked around the dining room. "Five nose rings, two shaved heads, and three kids with multiple piercings. Seems like a normal enough high school group to me. I think he blends in pretty well."

Paris grinned. "My hair's only been blue since yesterday," he explained. "Until then it was blonde. My family hates alternative anything, so I sprang the latest Kool-Aid job last night, just to freak 'em out."

Darrell finished the last of her lasagne and dropped her fork with a clatter. "Anyway, your name is stranger than your hair," she said, her voice muffled as she wiped tomato sauce from her mouth. "Who ever heard of a guy called Paris?"

Paris's grin widened. "Who ever heard of a girl called Darrell?" he shot back good-naturedly. "You need to bone up on your ancient Greek history," he added. "Paris was a famous hero who fought a war for his girlfriend, Helen of Troy."

"Darrell! I can't believe you didn't know that!" cried Kate, and looked at Paris with mock consternation. "She may look like an artist, but she has a secret interest in history, particularly late fourteenth-century Scotland, right Darrell?"

Darrell frowned. "Shut up, Kate. Leave my historical interests out of —"

"Shhh!" Brodie interrupted the argument. "It looks like the principal has something to say."

Professor Myrtle Tooth stood at the teachers' table, cleared her throat, and waited for silence. As soon as the voices filling the room died away, she began to speak in quiet, measured tones.

"Now that classes are underway, I would like to introduce a significant undertaking for the students of Eagle Glen School this term. We will celebrate the completion of exams by staging a Renaissance fair, to be held in the final days before winter break. All students will be expected to participate in some element of the fair, each to his own strength. Teachers will have comprehensive sign-up lists for each form. Fourth form will be responsible for the actual design and planning of the fair, accurate to historical detail whenever possible. Third form will be responsible for the construction required for the various events. Second form will help to organize scheduling, and first form will staff assigned stations as needed."

Professor Tooth swept the silent room with a glance. "The primary objective of this fair is to put into practical use the lessons presented about the Renaissance era during this term. Your form teachers will be available to further enlighten you on the details of this most important and entertaining event over the course of the next few weeks." She glanced at her watch. "And now, I do believe the first session of study hall has begun. You may proceed to your study rooms or feel free to continue your work here, as you see fit."

The scraping of chairs and a low murmur of conversation rose as students settled in with their first day's homework or left the dining hall for the smaller and more comfortable study rooms designated one to each school class.

"D'you want to stay here to work or move upstairs?" asked Kate.

Paris got to his feet. "Well, I'm going to the music room to practise," he said, as he shouldered a bulky instrument bag, "so I'll see you later, okay?"

Darrell nodded and smiled her goodbye. When Paris had strolled out of the room she glanced at Brodie. "Might be easier to talk here," he said in a low voice.

"The first- and second-form study rooms have an adjoining door, but I think less people can hear us here."

The tables around theirs had emptied and voices dropped to a muted murmur as the remaining students settled down to work.

"So — is Conrad in any of your classes?" whispered Darrell. "Paris says he has him in music."

Brodie nodded. "From the look of my classes today, it seems like grade level is less important than interest in the subject matter. I had kids from all of the forms in every one of my classes."

Kate pulled out a leaflet from her binder. "You're right, Brodie. It says here the teachers will establish individual learning outcomes for each student, and evaluation will be based on the outcomes."

"I guess that's how Conrad can be in our Renaissance history class when he's three years older than we are," Darrell added glumly.

"I'll bet Conrad's there so Professor Tooth can keep an eye on him," said Brodie shrewdly.

The sound of a dry cough made them all look up. "Completed your work, have you, Mr. Sun?"

Mr. Dickerman, Brodie's homeroom and archaeology teacher, was looking pointedly at Brodie's closed books.

"Oh, yes, well — we're getting right to it, sir," Brodie said, flipping open his notebook. Darrell smiled to herself. It had been a long time since she'd had a group of friends to study with. She cracked the spine of her new history text, and the three of them bent their heads to the task at hand.

CHAPTER THREE

The following week passed in a rush of classes, meeting new students, and a dizzying amount of work to do. Expectations were high, and most out-of-class time was spent working on projects and assignments. To her relief, Darrell found the only class she shared with Conrad was the Renaissance history class, and her worry about being around him lessened.

The weather continued to worsen as September moved into October, with blustery wind adding interest to the rain. The armchairs by the fire in the first-floor study came into high demand. Darrell was curled up reading her history text when Kate stuck her head into the room.

"You'd better get a move on, Darrell. We've got history in five minutes."

Darrell glanced at the already darkening sky through the window and then down at her watch.

"Okay, I'm coming." She stood up and grabbed her books.

Kate held the study door open. "Have you seen Paris anywhere? He's got my textbook."

Darrell shook her head. "He's probably in the class-room." But when they stepped into the class moments later, Paris wasn't anywhere to be seen.

Darrell dropped her books onto her desk. "He's probably just lost track of time. I'll go check the music room and you check the library."

Kate nodded. "If you find him, make sure he brings my textbook, okay?" She peeled out of the room and along the hall, while Darrell headed quickly down the stairs. She entered the music room to find Conrad taunting Paris, whose hair was now a vibrant shade of purple, in one corner of the room.

"Hey rich kid, nice hair."

"Thanks. Glad you like it. And I wish I was."

Conrad sneered. "Wish you were what?"

"Rich. Actually, I am feeling pretty loaded today. I've got twenty bucks burning a hole in my pocket, but I'll probably save it for the next time I go into town."

Darrell was getting used to seeing Conrad in the halls or in class, but the fear that rose in the back of her throat made her angry at herself every time. She frowned and took a step forward. "You coming to his-tory, Paris?" she asked. "I thought you might've lost track of the time, and Kate needs her text back."

Conrad sneered at Darrell. "Get lost, Gimpy. I hear your teacher calling you." He turned and dropped his voice to a whisper. "I can think of better ways to spend that money than you can, you purple-haired freak."

"What are you talking about?" Paris's expression became wary. Darrell took another cautious step into the room.

"Just what I said. Now hand it over." Conrad swivelled his head around and glared at Darrell. "You still here, Gimpy?"

Paris raised his eyebrows and turned to pick up his guitar, a look of cautious amusement on his face. "You've got to be kidding!" He bent down and unplugged the guitar from a small amplifier.

Conrad's face turned ugly. "Don't turn your back on me, you geek."

Paris began to load his instrument into its case, ignoring Conrad.

Conrad pushed aside a music stand and stepped forward. In one smooth motion he spun Paris by the shoulders and grabbed the front of his shirt. "This room is soundproofed, you doorknob," he hissed through his teeth. "And nobody can hear any kind of noise you make. So, I think that money's mine, now." With one hand still holding Paris's collar, he reached into the front pocket of his shirt and used two fingers to withdraw a twenty-dollar bill.

Paris went red to the roots of his purple hair. "Hey, you jerk! That's mine! Give it back." He reached over to grab the money, but Conrad leapt nimbly over a music stand. Darrell felt sick as she watched from the door. *You're a lot of help, you big chicken.*

"I don't see your name on it," drawled Conrad as he elbowed Paris aside and turned to leave.

Darrell gathered her courage. "I do," she said, stalling for time and not knowing what else to say. Conrad sneered at her and opened his mouth to speak.

"So do I."

Conrad closed his mouth with a snap and turned to look at the stage door.

Kate stepped into the room. A tiny smile played at the corner of her mouth. "Hey Connie. You being a bully again?"

Conrad glared at Kate but swallowed nervously. His eyes flitted back and forth among the people in the room, assessing.

"Need a girl to fight your battles, do ya?" he taunted Paris.

Some of the normal colour returned to Paris's face. "Is it going to be a battle, then, Conrad?" he asked quietly.

"That — that's not what I meant," Conrad spluttered.

"Do I scare you, Connie?" asked Kate, innocence radiating from every pore. She took another step forward.

Conrad's will broke. He took the twenty out of his pocket and stuffed it back into Paris's shirt. He kicked a music stand out of his way and stomped to the stage door.

"Get out of my way," he snarled to Kate, who stood her ground in front of the door.

"You didn't say please," she said casually and reached out towards Conrad's shirt.

His eyes wild, Conrad tore his shirt from Kate's grasp and ran out of the room, slamming the door.

"He seemed in a bit of a hurry," noted Kate, to no one in particular.

Paris exhaled rather shakily. "Thanks, you two. I think you helped save me twenty bucks right there."

Darrell shook her head. "I wasn't any help."

Paris glanced at Kate. "Conrad seemed pretty nervous around you." He looked at her small frame disbelievingly. "You don't look very scary to me."

Darrell laughed. "I never go anywhere without her," she said. "She might look small but she's pretty feisty."

"Feisty? Try fit, fast, and frightening," Kate said with a grin. She dropped her hands to the ground, did a quick handstand, and flipped back onto her feet in front of Paris.

"Okay, okay," he said, laughing. "You've convinced me. Karate, right?"

"Nope. Tae kwon do. A very similar martial art, though," she said, and her face took on a distant expression. "You just use the opposite side of the body. The theory is a bit different, too..."

"Okay, Paris, don't get her started or she'll go on for hours," said Darrell. "So what really happened?"

Paris frowned. "I was finishing practice when Conrad came in. He didn't even touch his own guitar. Just accused me of being a rich kid and then tried to take my money."

Kate's nodded shrewdly. "I knew that leopard wouldn't change his spots," she said, her voice warming with anger. She turned back to Paris. "The guy is a total jerk, and extortion is no joke."

"I can handle it." Paris swung his guitar case onto his shoulder. "I'm on to him now."

Kate shrugged as they walked out the door of the music room. "Lucky it's history we're late for," she said with a grin. "Do you think Professor Tooth will be interested in our excuse?"

Paris shook his head. "Hey, this is my problem and I'll deal with it, okay?" He looked from Kate's face to Darrell's. "Don't say anything to the principal. I'll handle Conrad."

Darrell shrugged. "If you say so. I don't think it's going to help, though. Conrad's just going to get worse."

"We'll see," said Paris. He grabbed his backpack and led the way out the door.

The following Saturday dawned clear and cool with signs in the sky of a beautiful late October day. Darrell lay in bed looking through the large, curved glass window that formed a part of the tower wall. It gently distorted the view outside, magnifying the sky into an unending plane of pale, clear blue.

The door flung back on its hinges as Lily bounded into the room. Her wet hair was knotted into an untidy tangle on top of her head and she dropped a large pile of wet clothes and towels into a heap on the floor. "I can't believe you guys are still asleep! I've already been swimming for an hour and I'm starving."

The smell of peppermint shampoo seeped through Darrell's sleep-muddled brain. She frowned at Lily's back and peeked over at Kate's bed. A tousled red head emerged for a moment from under the covers and then disappeared under a pillow. Lily shook her head disapprovingly and glanced at her watch. "Kate Clancy, if you didn't stay up so late playing computer games, you'd be able to enjoy this beautiful morning."

No response.

"Did you hear me, Kate?" Lily persisted.

A gentle snore was the only reply. Lily sighed and rolled her eyes. "Nothing's changed from the summer term, I can see."

Darrell sat up in bed and mustered a weak smile.

"Oh, well. It's her loss. I'm going down for breakfast." Lily threw a wet sock at Darrell, her good humour restored. "Join me?"

"No thanks. I'm still a bit sleepy. I think I'll wait for Kate."

"Whatever." Lily scooped up her laundry and headed briskly for the hall, closing the door behind her with a shade more energy than was strictly required.

"Is she gone?" The muffled words emerged from the tumbled pile of covers on Kate's bed.

"Yeah."

"Thank God. She is altogether too cheerful in the morning. At least you need to have coffee before you start being so loud."

"I'm never that loud!" Darrell replied indignantly. "And the good thing about Lily and her early mornings is she is always asleep before eight o'clock at night. Leaves us free to do other things."

Kate emerged, rubbing her eyes. "Such as?"

"Well, the sun's out. Feel like a hike?"

Kate groaned. "First Lily, then you. Who's responsible for all this energy around here?"

Darrell swung her legs over the bed and reached for her prosthesis. "The truth is, Brodie suggested that we go back to the cave for a look around today. And it's finally stopped raining."

Kate peered blearily through the window. "I should have known the fossil geek was behind this." She glanced shrewdly back at Darrell. "Have you been planning this for long?"

Darrell shook her head. "Between homework and worrying about who Conrad is going to pick on next, I haven't had time to think about anything else. But Brodie suggested it last night, and, well, the idea has kind of grown on me." She paused with her hand on the dresser drawer. "I even dreamed about it last night."

"You did?" Kate suddenly looked a great deal less sleepy.

"Yeah. It was weird. I dreamt we went into the cave and when we came out we could all fly!"

"What's weird about that? I'm always dreaming about flying. I just put out my arms and soar. It's really cool."

"Yeah, I have those dreams, too. But last night, we were flying some kind of strange machine. It looked like a kite crossed with one of those old-fashioned biplanes."

"Okay, I guess that is strange."

Darrell sighed and rubbed her eyes. "I dreamt Brodie was hurt, too. I think he fell out of the plane, or something. Anyway, he had blood on his face. So I'm glad Lily woke me."

"Oh, you're probably just excited. That gives me bad dreams, sometimes. We haven't been back to the cave since August. I wonder if there will be any new glyphs."

Darrell shook her head doubtfully. "I've been there since you have, remember? I met Professor Tooth there when I went back for — for a final look at the end of the summer." She stared out the window at the pale blue of the fall sky. "I was so disappointed because there wasn't anything left. Just the burnt shapes of the three glyphs from the summer. Nothing else."

"Well, it will still be fun to go back in there. Maybe Brodie can get pictures of the glyphs to send to his friend at the university. Who knows? We might be able to figure out how it all happened."

Darrell smiled. "I doubt it. Glyphs that glowed and pulled us back through time? No one will ever believe us, let alone explain what happened." She grabbed her towel and strode purposefully to the door. "Anyway, I want to go see the cave today even if only to remember how amazing it was. I'm going to have a quick shower first. Meet you outside in ten minutes."

As she headed for the shower, Darrell caught a glimpse of Kate's head as it slipped back onto the pillow. She stopped in the doorway and listened to Kate's sleepy muttering.

"Ten minutes," Kate said, her voice still gravelly. "Good. That gives me eight more minutes of sleep." She pulled the covers over her head and sighed with contentment. Darrell laughed out loud and ran for the shower.

Darrell and Kate stood in the small garden behind the school, waiting for Brodie. Delaney lifted his head and sniffed the breeze, tail fanning gently. Kate's hair rose like a messy red halo around her head, contrasting sharply with Darrell's neat chestnut ponytail.

"Nice job with the hairbrush this morning," Darrell teased.

Kate grinned and stuffed her hands in her pockets. "It's all Lily's fault. Her infernal cheerfulness drives me further under the covers."

They were both laughing as Brodie stepped out of the side door of the school.

"Sorry I'm late," he said, clinking, "but I wanted to be prepared."

"That's the understatement of the year," said Darrell, exchanging a glance with Kate. "The last time you lugged so much gear I lost you for a few days, if you recall."

Brodie had a full pack on his back, a baseball cap stuck backwards on his head, and one of his new tap hammers clutched in his hand. The pack dangled with instruments, including small picks for rocks and fossils, a compass, several varieties of flashlights, and a small hurricane lantern. A large army knife was snugged into its pouch at his belt and a headlamp was strapped around the ballcap on his head.

"You look ready for a two-week trip to the Carlsbad Caverns," Kate said, her eyes wide with disbelief. "All this to take a few pictures?"

Brodie grinned. "Always pays to be prepared," he said, striding off across the lawn. "Are you guys going to wait around all day? Let's get going!"

Darrell and Kate caught up quickly and Delaney led the trio down the curving path to the beach.

"Thought you might be interested in a little conversation I just had with Mrs. Follett," Brodie said, as they made their way down the steep path.

Kate raised an eyebrow. "An interesting conversation? That'll be a first. I don't think I've ever heard an interesting word come out of that woman's mouth. 'Where are your registration forms, Ms. Clancy?' 'Did you remember your inoculation records, Ms. Clancy?'"

Brodie grinned. "You are a nasty piece of work this morning! Must have had an early wake-up call from Lily."

Kate stuck out her tongue as they stepped off the path onto the beach.

"Mrs. Follett doesn't have to be interesting to do her job as school secretary," said Darrell. "Besides, she knows everything that goes on around here. What did she say to you?" Darrell turned to hear Brodie's story.

"I popped into the office to grab a field trip form, and Mrs. Follett was talking on the phone. I heard her say: 'She's got to be somewhere. As soon as you find her, please have her contact the school.' I didn't want her to think I was eavesdropping —"

"Even though you were," interrupted Kate.

"— so I cleared my throat as she was hanging up the phone," Brodie continued. "She looked so startled to see me, I asked her if everything was okay, and she said 'Of course it is,' handed me my form, and practically pushed me out the door."

"So what's interesting?" Kate said, using the rocks littering the beach as stepping stones.

"I bet I know," Darrell added. "It was Conrad she was talking about, right?"

Brodie nodded. "His mother, I think. His file was wide open on the counter."

Kate stopped her balancing act on the rocks and planted her feet in the sand. "His dad's in jail and his mother's missing. Some life that kid's got."

"Y'know," said Darrell, her voice heated, "some of us have awful lives but don't turn into complete jerks."

"I never said you were a complete jerk," said Kate, grinning. "Just a little jerk, that's all." She took off like a rabbit, leaping over rocks as Darrell and Delaney chased her down the beach.

Out of breath and good humour restored, they followed the shoreline, Darrell setting the pace with her unique hop-skip stride. Brodie struggled along beside Kate.

"For a girl with only one leg, you move pretty fast," he said good-naturedly.

Darrell turned around and flashed him a grin. She dropped back beside her friends.

"I guess I'm kind of excited. Even though I know it's all over, walking this way still reminds me of last summer."

"I'm *glad* it's all over," said Kate. "I still don't understand most of what happened. We were very lucky things turned out as well as they did. Conrad might have caught you in the cave, Darrell, and his dad is a very violent man. It could have been a nightmare." She glanced over her shoulder.

Brodie laughed. "You look as though you are expecting him to jump out from behind a rock," he said. "I checked. He's off on some kind of a family visit with his dad at the prison. He'll be away for the whole weekend."

"Anyway," Darrell added, "he's out of our hair for now. And there are no more glyphs on the cave walls. This is only a visit to get Brodie's pictures."

They circled the last group of large, standing rocks and carefully picked their way to the mouth of the cave. A salty tang in the air came from a fresh breeze blowing off the water. There were a few difficult moments as Brodie discovered that his pack, even off his back, was too wide to fit through the narrow slit in the rock serving as the door to the cave. Darrell and Kate did a small amount of repacking and a large amount of grumbling while Delaney wagged his tail and barked his impatience. After several sweaty moments of effort, Brodie and his pack finally squeezed into the cave.

Once inside, Brodie switched on his headlamp and handed flashlights to the girls. They flicked on their lights and made a slow inventory of the cave entrance.

"Everything looks the same in here," said Kate.

"Let's keep moving then," suggested Brodie.

The temperature was warmer inside the cave than on the beach, but the air was dank and stale. Darrell walked along in silence, listening to the gentle echoes stirred up by their passage. The roof dropped lower as they neared the back. Brodie hunched his shoulders.

"You must have grown a bit since we were last here," remarked Kate. "I don't remember you having to duck before…" Her words ended in a loud gasp, and she pointed at the cave wall. "Look!" she whispered. "There's a new glyph!"

Darrell and Brodie hustled over to the wall. Darrell cursed herself silently. *Why didn't I clean off the red chalk the day I met Professor Tooth in the cave?*

"What do you think it is, Brodie?" Kate peered at the image in the beam of the flashlight.

Darrell stepped forward, hoping her suddenly reddened cheeks wouldn't show in the glow of her friends' flashlights. "Remember I told you I came back to the cave on the last day of summer school?" she asked. "I met Professor Tooth in here and she told me the school had been licensed and we could all come back in the fall."

Brodie and Kate both nodded.

"Well, what I didn't tell you is why I came." Darrell hung her head and fiddled with her flashlight for a moment, the beam zigzagging wildly along the walls. Kate reached over and took the flashlight from Darrell's hands.

"Let me guess," she said quietly, pointing the flashlight at the new glyph. "I see a man, a girl, and a motorbike with a flat tire." She turned back and peered at Darrell's face in the shadows.

"You were trying to go back, right? To the time of your accident?"

Darrell nodded miserably. "I thought I might be able to change things — to have my whole leg again — to bring him back, maybe."

"But you didn't draw the other glyphs, did you?" Brodie sounded puzzled.

Darrell shook her head. "No, of course not." She traced a finger along the cool rock wall. "I brought some red chalk I found in the art room. I was hoping the cave walls held whatever magic I needed to take me back. If I could find a way to harness the magic, maybe I could direct myself back in time and change my life to the way it should be."

They stood silent, lights carefully directed away from Darrell's sketch. Brodie got out his camera and took a couple of pictures of the blackened glyphs, now little more than charred smears on the rock. "These are never going to turn out," he complained. "There really isn't anything left to take a picture of."

After a few moments, Darrell walked to the other wall and brushed the chalk dust off with her hands. Her sketch, already smudged, blurred into a red smear on the rock. She cleared her throat.

"That's that," she said. "Professor Tooth got here just as I realized my own artwork had no magic to it. She told me even *she* didn't know why things happen the way they do." Darrell shook her head. "I guess I'm stuck with this stupid leg after all."

Kate walked along the opposite wall of the cave, shining her light on the glistening surface. "I think you're wrong, Darrell," she said, her voice a jumble of gentle echoes. "Your drawings do have magic in them. Maybe not the same kind of magic that sent us through the wall into the fourteenth century, but they are magical in a different way." She paused. "Did you do this one, too? It looks like one of yours."

Darrell was puzzled. "No, only the one I brushed away."

Brodie stepped over to Kate's side. He pointed his flashlight at the spot on the wall and his headlamp bobbed, making the image dance.

"Hold your head still, Brodie," commanded Darrell, as she looked over his shoulder. The three gazed in silence at a small picture drawn onto the rock wall of the cave.

"It's a lighthouse," said Kate.

"Not just any lighthouse," said Brodie, excitement in his voice. "It's the lighthouse on the point at the other end of the beach. See the checkerboard pattern painted around the base?"

"I'm sure lots of lighthouses have a similar pattern," muttered Darrell. "But it really does look like our lighthouse and I most definitely did not draw it."

Brodie pulled out his camera and snapped a couple of pictures. He reached over to touch one corner of the drawing. "This looks like it's the same chalk you used, Darrell. It doesn't seem like the other glyphs at all."

Darrell traced one finger across the corner of the lighthouse. The surface smudged under her touch.

Kate looked around and shifted her weight from foot to foot. "Someone must have found our cave," she said anxiously. "Let's head back out, okay?" She tugged on Darrell's arm and started back.

Brodie looked at Kate with some exasperation, his headlamp making her blink as he strode along beside her. "It's not *our* cave, Kate. It's been here for thousands of years before we were born and it will probably be here for thousands of years after we die."

"This isn't making me feel any better," said Kate. "*Someone* drew that lighthouse."

"I've got an idea," Brodie said with a grin. "What about if we make our next expedition aboveground? Let's go to the lighthouse and check it out."

"Anything to get out of this place," Kate answered. "It gives me the creeps."

Darrell, trailing behind, didn't answer. They walked awhile without talking, and the filtered grey light grew brighter as they approached the entrance. The distant cry of a seabird echoed mournfully in the cave.

They managed with some difficulty to pull Brodie's pack through the crack at the entrance to the cave, and then sat down outside on the warm sand.

"Have you got any food in that thing?" inquired Kate. "Now that we're out of that creepy place, I'm suddenly starving."

"I told you I was prepared," said Brodie, pulling out a large container of crackers and cheese. "Let's grab something to eat and then hike over to the lighthouse."

Kate grinned and opened the container. "Nice to know you're good for something other than crawling around underground," she said, her mouth full. She glanced over Darrell's shoulder. "Oh-oh."

Darrell looked up and saw Paris hiking along the beach with Lily in tow. "Looks like our trip to the light-house might not work out after all."

Kate brushed cracker crumbs off her shirt. "Not if we want to go alone."

"Hey," Paris said, puffing a little as he strode up. "We were going for a hike and then spotted you guys down here."

"This is great," Lily said, beaming. "A picnic!" She plopped down on the sand beside Kate and helped herself to a few crackers.

"Yeah — yeah, just great," said Brodie, rolling his eyes.

Darrell, resigned, leaned back against a warm rock. Lily's cheerful chatter faded away as Darrell, lost in her own thoughts, stared unseeing into the mouth of the cave and rubbed the rusty red dust between her fingers.

CHAPTER FOUR

On Friday after school, Darrell, Kate, and Brodie set off for the lighthouse. The sky was grey and threatening, but the rain held off. The wind blew icy gusts across the water, and the tips of the waves were crowned a foaming white. Brodie's heavy pack made walking in the sand along the shore difficult, so the small group opted to follow the rockier but more firmly packed sand along the cliff edge.

"This way should keep us out of sight of the school," noted Darrell, glancing back.

"More out of the wind, too." Kate pulled up and fastened her hood.

Darrell picked her way among the rocks, Delaney close at her heels. The firmer sand was easier for her to walk on, too, and she remembered the last time she had been down to this end of the beach. A gull soared high above, a white spot of fluff on a blanket-grey sky.

She gestured at the small spit sticking out like an accusing finger into the waters of the sound. "I don't see any illegal activities going on here today," she said with a smile.

"Now that his dad's gone to jail, I haven't seen Conrad near the beach at all this year," Brodie said, hitching his pack more comfortably onto his shoulders.

Kate shivered. "He'd have to be crazy to come down here in this weather." She turned her back to the wind and tried to walk backwards, but immediately tripped on a rock and just managed to keep her feet.

Darrell scooped up a stick to throw for Delaney, and he chased it, barking joyfully, down the beach. They followed the curve of the cliffs until they reached the south end of the stretch of beach, and then began to scramble along the rocks.

"As lighthouses go, this one seems pretty small," said Kate, one foot slithering along the slippery rocks.

"What would you know about it? I haven't seen you burying yourself in local history lately," Brodie said, laughing.

Kate looked impatient. "Okay, so maybe not local history. But Ainslie Castle has sure given me a taste for Professor Tooth's Renaissance class," she retorted. "And after finding that sketch in the cave, I spent some time on the Internet, researching everything I could about lighthouses. Most of the ones on the west coast are no longer manned by keepers." She reached with a gloved hand to grasp a rock at the base of the tower and hoisted herself up.

"Can you take this?" Brodie handed up his pack and Delaney jumped over the sharp edge to stand beside

Kate. Brodie climbed up and turned to grab Darrell's hand, hauling her over the last few rocks and onto the flat base around the lighthouse.

"I wouldn't want that job," added Brodie, puffing a little. "Too lonely for my taste."

"Actually, there was a lot of protest when the lighthouses were automated," Kate went on. "They usually have fog horns, too, so it's better if there's a keeper around to handle things when they break down."

The area immediately around the base of the lighthouse was lined with a flat path of pea gravel and covered in crushed mussel shells. Delaney led the way around to the seaward side. "So how come there's no one running this one?" asked Darrell curiously.

"Well, by the time everyone realized the lighthouse keepers were an endangered species, they had already been mostly phased out. This one was shut down in 1978."

"Wow." Brodie looked at Kate with admiration. "I guess the little box you spend all your time staring at sometimes does help you find something worthwhile."

Kate grinned and punched him lightly on the arm. "Shut up. Here's the door."

Darrell touched a shiny padlock dangling from a well-rusted chain. The chain circled through a pair of old bolts in the wall.

"What do you make of this?" said Darrell, turning over the padlock in her hands.

"Looks new. Maybe the Parks people who maintain the lighthouse attached it," Kate offered.

"Maybe so," said Brodie doubtfully, "but I think it may have something to do with this sign." He gestured at a tattered notice, wrapped in plastic and tacked on three corners to a wooden board on the wall. One corner of the notice was torn and flapping in the wind. Darrell held it down with a gloved hand. It read: *Demolition Permit.*

"The date's torn off," Darrell remarked.

"And why would someone put a brand new lock on such a rusty old chain?" asked Kate. "Wouldn't they replace both?"

"Something's going on here," said Brodie. "Look at this."

He indicated a small pile of cylindrical objects near the door. Darrell and Kate bent down to examine them more closely.

"Looks like shotgun shells," Darrell said at last.

"But this is the edge of a national park. Animals and birds are protected here, aren't they?" asked Kate.

"Yup. No guns allowed," said Brodie. "But maybe someone's been shooting at seabirds."

"Well, if that's so, whoever left these shell casings could still be around here," said Kate. "Maybe they use the lighthouse as a base, or something." She poked Darrell with a gloved finger. "Maybe Conrad's up to his old tricks."

Brodie shrugged. "Well, like I said, I haven't seen him down here at all lately."

"And how much time have you been spending here yourself?" Kate asked, triumphant.

"Whoever put this here wasn't very bright," said Darrell, examining the lock and chain.

Kate and Brodie stepped closer. The rusty chain was threaded through the handle of the door, but there was no functioning lock on the door itself, and it hung loose from a single hinge.

"The old chain is locked on securely enough," she continued, "but if you follow the chain into this little doorwell, you can see the end is —"

"Not attached!" Brodie concluded. "Let's go in."

"I don't know..." said Kate.

Darrell leaned her back against the lighthouse wall. "Let's think about this for a minute," she said, looking at Brodie. "Breaking and entering isn't usually your style."

Brodie laughed. "It's not really 'breaking' if we just unhook the end of the chain," he said. "I only want to have a quick look around and then we can go."

Darrell nodded. "Yeah, Brodie's right. We won't touch anything, Kate. We'll take a fast look around inside to see if we can figure out who's been here, and then we'll leave. I don't want to hang around either."

Delaney pushed past Darrell, nosed the door open, and slipped inside.

"Hey, Delaney!" Darrell called, sticking her face in the dark doorway.

"Well, I guess we've got to get the dog back," said Kate. "But just a quick peek, okay?"

One hand shading his eyes, Brodie looked towards the shore. "I'd feel better about this if the entrance was on the seaward side," he said quietly. "But I think it's too cold up on the cliffs for anyone to be sitting around watching us. Because this lock is in place, I think it's obvious whoever put it here is gone. All the same," he indicated the shoreline with a shrug of his shoulders, "there are a lot of hills up there. Lots of places to hide."

Kate shivered. "Okay, you're right. I change my mind. Let's call Delaney and go back to the school."

"Kate!" Darrell's voice was impatient. "We'll only go in for a minute or two and then head straight back to report these shotgun casings, I promise."

Kate scanned the hillside. She narrowed her eyes at Brodie and followed Darrell under the chain. "Okay, but I'm timing you. Two minutes!" Brodie passed his backpack though the opening and followed the girls inside. He pushed the door shut with a creak behind them and three flashlights clicked on, beams piercing the darkness.

They stood in a small entryway that served as a landing for a flight of wooden steps spiralling upwards into the gloom.

"This must be where the lighthouse keepers hung their wet clothes," whispered Darrell. A number of hooks were nailed haphazardly along the wall, and in several places where they had fallen out altogether, the hooks had been replaced by rusty spikes driven into the wall at intervals.

"There doesn't seem to be room for much else in here," remarked Brodie. "Let's take a quick peek upstairs." Before Kate had a chance to protest, he clambered up the wooden steps, flashlight bobbing.

"Careful," Darrell panted, following him. "One of the boards is broken." She pointed out the spot with her flashlight, and the beam was swallowed by darkness inside the jagged hole. They stepped over the riser entirely and in a moment they circled to the top of the first flight of stairs.

"Agh. All the spinning makes me feel sick," complained Kate, putting her hand on Darrell's shoulder to steady herself.

"Try not to wear yourself out, Action Girl," Brodie said, grinning.

Kate stuck out her tongue.

"We'll be going back down the other direction in a minute," said Darrell, practically, "so your head will have a chance to even itself out."

Brodie paced the perimeter of the round room. "I think this must have been the main living area for the lighthouse keeper," he said, using his flashlight to examine the floor as he took each step.

Darrell walked past Kate, who was leaning against a wall, and began to examine the place herself. "Looks like there have been a few people here since the lighthouse closed down," she remarked, indicating a pile of wrappers and chip bags strewn to one side.

"Yeah," said Kate. "This place is a pigsty."

Darrell gestured with her flashlight at the worn wooden boards on the floor. "Don't see any of those shell casings in here, though."

"I'd like to remind you *we* are the trespassers this time," said Kate in a worried tone. "So could you hurry up?" She slid back along the wall towards Darrell and disappeared with a yell.

"Kate!" chorused Brodie and Darrell, and rushed across the room.

"It's okay — I mean — I'm okay," came a muffled voice. To Darrell's relief, Kate's smudged face appeared in the beam of her flashlight. Darrell reached down to help Kate to her feet.

"What happened?" demanded Brodie.

"I — I was leaning on the wall and then I guess I took a step to the side. I think one of the floorboards must be broken and I tripped and fell because the wall wasn't there anymore."

Brodie gave a low chuckle, relief in his voice. "I think you may have stumbled into the anteroom that leads up to the light, Kate." Three flashlight beams turned to illuminate a small opening in the outer wall of the room that led to a second, smaller stairwell. Brodie stuck his flashlight inside and the light reflected back from the surface of the lamp in the small room above. The reflection was so bright they all closed their eyes in pain.

"Don't do that, Brodie!" Darrell's voice was taut with alarm. "Someone is sure to see the reflection of your flashlight."

"Guys, we really should get out of here now." Kate's voice had taken on a panicky edge. "I don't want to get caught in here, especially when someone has had a gun here recently."

"One minute." Brodie thundered up the tiny staircase and was back down again before Kate or Darrell could protest. "It's okay. The reflector was pointing out to the water. It doesn't rotate anymore, so I don't think anyone on the land could have seen it." He paused. "All the same, I think Kate is right. It's time for us to get out of here."

Delaney brushed against Darrell's knee and headed up the staircase.

"Time to go, boy," called Darrell, but Delaney stood on the step and barked again. Darrell followed him up through the heavy wooden door at the top of the stairs. "I'm just going to have a quick look from the top," she yelled.

"Let's go, Darrell," called Kate, her voice a tremulous mix of nerves and exasperation. No answer. Brodie shrugged and the two raced up the stairs behind Darrell and Delaney.

"It's too dark outside to see anything much now," complained Kate, her nose pressed against the glass of the lantern room. "We'd better be getting back to the school before it's too hard to find our way along the beach."

The last light of day formed a red line above the mountains to the west and the trio gazed out at it in silence. Delaney pushed his head under Darrell's hand and whined.

"What's bothering you, boy?" Darrell asked. The wind had picked up outside, and the waves were smashing white foam against the base of the lighthouse. Water seemed to be lifting from the surface of the sea and mixing with the rain that had finally started to fall. The glass of the lantern chamber became a haze of tiny droplets.

"The storm has moved in pretty fast," said Brodie. "I can't see a thing out there."

"Look you two, we've got the dog — let's go, okay?" pleaded Kate.

"Okay, but let's keep the flashlights off, just in case," said Darrell.

"You'd better grab my hand then, Darrell," said Kate, clutching Brodie's jacket as he started down.

Darrell nodded. Curling her fingers in Delaney's collar, she followed Brodie and Kate down the twisting staircase. A sudden gust tore up through the stairwell, causing the door above them to slam shut. Kate clung to Darrell's hand tightly. "Where's this wind coming from?" she gasped. Darrell opened her mouth to reply, but her words were blown back down her throat as a maelstrom swept her away.

CHAPTER FIVE

I've been here before. Darrell tried to lift her head to look around, but groaned quietly and rolled into a ball instead. Her body was wracked with nausea, her head felt as though it had been split like a piece of firewood, and even her eyeballs hurt. Sure knowledge crept around the edges of her misery, but she pushed all thought away and focused on what little light she could see. The darkness was cut by thin, golden threads in the shape of a tall rectangle hovering like a halo at some indeterminate distance. A door? She heard a scuffling beside her and straightened her neck to try to see the source.

I've felt like this before. A large rat scuttled over and peered into her face.

"Agh!" Headache or not, she wasn't prepared to face down a rat under any circumstances. At the sound of her voice, the rat scampered across the straw-covered floor, and as Darrell leapt up, understanding swept through her like a flood.

Delaney gave a low growl as he scrambled to chase the rat. Darrell grabbed the dog as he ran past and dropped to one knee. Holding his large head in both hands, she searched his face in the gloom.

"Does he look the same?" Brodie's voice croaked behind her.

Darrell turned, the nausea making her head spin. "Well, it might be the light, but he looks pretty brown to me. Are you okay?"

Brodie had rolled onto his hands and knees, a shadow in the dark room. "Yeah. Lucky I had some candy in my pocket." He crawled over and placed a small mint in Darrell's hand.

The sweet mint filled Darrell's mouth and pushed the nausea back almost immediately. "I can't believe it," she whispered. "It's happened again."

Brodie nodded. "Different clothes this time." As Darrell's eyes adjusted, she could see Brodie's long legs were encased in some kind of red hose, and he wore an elaborate tunic, belted at the waist.

"Tights?" Amusement tempered Darrell's shock.

Kate groaned and Brodie stepped to her side in one stride. "Have one of these," he whispered, and helped her roll up. Darrell slid along the floor to get closer to Kate, clothing forgotten for the moment.

Kate held one hand to her forehead as if to keep her brain lodged safely inside. "My head..." she began, and then, through the dim light, Darrell saw her eyes snap open wide. "Oh *no*," she whispered, as she looked around, moving her head tentatively. "Are we back in Mallaig?"

Darrell stepped towards the thin lines of light, which indeed delineated a door. "I'm not sure *where* we are, Katie," she whispered. "But we're not in the lighthouse anymore."

As Darrell reached the door, it swung open, and she squeezed her eyes against the brilliance and staggered back. A figure stood in the doorway, a corona of sunlight bathing his silhouette in molten gold. It was impossible to more than glance at the dazzling figure, but the image was burned into Darrell's retina the instant she closed her aching eyes.

Brodie stepped between the door and the spot where Darrell stood leaning against a wooden beam. Darrell cracked her eyes open and could see Brodie's face, grim with determination. His skin was pale in the reflected light.

"Brodie," she rasped, her throat still sore, "be careful." Her eyes began gradually to adjust to the light, and she noticed the figure at the door hadn't moved. The person gazed long and hard into the stable.

Brodie cleared his throat. "We mean no harm," he said quietly. "We are just travellers seeking shelter."

Darrell heard Kate gasp at Brodie's words and silently implored her friend to keep quiet with a tiny shake of the head. Kate clapped her hand over her own mouth as if to stop herself from speaking and looked at Darrell with huge eyes.

The figure at the door moved for the first time, stepping inside and pushing the large door almost closed. The brilliant light lessened, though it continued to pour through the crack like melted butter.

"*Buon giorno*," said the young man. He looked pointedly around the stable in which they all stood. "I know who you are. But where are your mounts? And your carriage?"

Brodie's mouth opened and closed like a fish.

Darrell spoke out, though she could feel herself blushing. "We've —ah — sent them away.

The young man's face cleared. "I see. You have stabled them nearby, then?"

Darrell nodded, and the young man stepped away from the door and grasped Brodie by the shoulders. "I can see you do not recognize me — your own cousin — Giovanni Luca Clemente! It has been many years, and all I can see of you," he turned Brodie so the light shone onto his face and examined him critically, "must come from your mother's family. You have nothing of your father, my uncle, in you, it is plain. Nevertheless, allow me to welcome you, *Cugino* Bruno, to the home of Andrea Verrocchio! You will spend a fruitful season, studying under the master."

Darrell's heart pounded and she felt she must have heard incorrectly. "Surely," she stammered, "not *the* Verrocchio?"

"And none other, of course!" He laughed, standing tall, then turned back to Brodie. "Who were you expecting? Your father has apprenticed you for the season, has he not? He sent word to my family to expect you this week — and here you are!" He gestured dismissively at Darrell and Kate. "Send your serving girls to the kitchens and let me show you around."

Brodie raised his eyebrows at Darrell. "These are not servants — ah — Cousin Giovanni. They are…" he stumbled, as though the words had dried up in his mouth.

"Sisters of his friend," Darrell interjected, "who was unable to attend, though promised a place. We are here to study, too, in his stead. My name is Dara and this is — Katerina."

The young man laughed, loud and long, and slapped his knee in apparent delight. "*Girls*," he said, barely recovered, "girls do *not* study with Verrocchio." He looked at Kate appraisingly. "You'd better stay in the kitchens, with red hair and a name like Katerina."

Kate flushed. "What's that supposed to mean?"

He shrugged and grabbed Brodie by the sleeve. "Now come along, cousin. You have not been here since you were a tiny baby. I will show you around while the girls find their way to the *cucina*." With a yank on Brodie's arm, the young man pulled him out into the golden afternoon.

"Italian! We're speaking Italian." Kate was on her feet, pacing.

Darrell nodded. "Italian, or something very like it," she said. "The only Italian words I've heard are when my Uncle Frank drops a hammer on his toe, and he won't ever translate."

"Quit kidding around, Darrell. We need to follow them!" Kate said, her eyes frantic.

"Just a minute." Darrell sat down on the stable floor with a thud. She ran her hands over her clothes and patted the floor beside her. "Let's just take stock for a minute here, okay?"

Kate paced around the stable, biting a thumbnail. But when Delaney pushed his nose into her hand, she glanced down at him for a moment and then slumped on the straw beside Darrell. She rubbed her cheek against Delaney's soft head. "He's changed clothes too," she said, her lips curling into a tiny smile.

"He looks like he did on our trip to Mallaig," said Darrell, ruffling the dog's fur.

"He *is* brown, but his fur is longer and he's not as skinny as before."

Darrell winced at the memory of the starving dogs she had seen roaming the streets of Mallaig during the Black Plague. "It seems like, whenever this is, times are a bit better," she said. "Our clothes are richer, for one thing."

Kate looked down at her own dress, a floor-length tunic of a finely striped silk in vivid red and gold with rich brocade. "Yeah." She ran her hands along the lush fabric. "I don't feel quite so frightened this time," she said, her voice lower. "And this whole experience is different from the cave. How can a lighthouse turn into a stable?"

Darrell shrugged. "I don't know. It's almost like we were pulled through a doorway and landed here."

"That's not how it felt for me," Kate said, rubbing her head. "More like we'd been sucked into a giant blender, spun around a million or so times, and spat out on the floor."

Darrell pulled up the hem of her own elaborate overskirt and sighed. "One thing's certain," she said with a grimace, "they don't make prostheses much more comfortable here than they did in Scotland." The wooden peg bound tightly to her leg looked depressingly familiar, though the wood was of a fine grain and elaborately carved, ending in a roll-toed paw, similar to a piano leg.

Kate ran her hand down her own dress again. "I believe this is silk," she said, excitement in her voice, "but it feels a little draughty..."

Darrell grinned at the look of horror creeping over Kate's face. "Must be summertime," she said with satisfaction, "'cause I'm not wearing any underwear, and I bet you aren't either!"

"Darrell!" Kate jumped back to her feet, smoothing down her skirts. "We're going to have to do something about this!"

Darrell laughed out loud.

"Listen Kate, we've got more important things to worry about than the state of your underwear. And besides, can you imagine how Brodie feels? He looks like he's wearing a short skirt and tights!" She reached up a hand and Kate helped her stand.

Darrell tried to tuck a loose strand of hair behind her ear, but found her hair was caught up in two knots, one on either side of her head.

"Agh! Please tell me I don't look like Princess Leia."

Kate brushed the straw off her clothes. "No, you don't. In fact, it kinda suits you. I can't believe how heavy all these clothes are." She held out her voluminous skirts in a wide arc. "Some kind of brocade overskirt, silk dress, whatever this vest thingy is..."

"Now you know why there's no underwear. It's too hot!" Darrell laughed.

Kate undid her high-buttoned collar. "That's a bit better. Now you were talking about taking stock. Have you got a plan?"

Darrell shrugged. "Nope. Not yet. I think we need to get the lay of the land first. Now, considering that Giovanni guy was going to send us to the kitchen right away, I think you should hide out here with Delaney. Brodie will probably be back in a few minutes." She peeked into a nearby stall. "This stable doesn't look like it's being used at the moment, so hopefully no one will come in here for a while."

"Okay." Kate peered through the dim light. "But how do you know it's not being used?"

Darrell made a face. "Smell any horse manure? And the mangers are all empty."

"Okay," Kate repeated, "but don't be long. We need to figure out how to get back to school, now that we don't have a cave or glyphs or anything."

"We *do* have something going for us, Kate," said Darrell. "We have Delaney. And we have our brains and our wits. We'll figure it out."

Kate looked unconvinced.

"I'm just going to have a quick look around. I'll be back in ten minutes, tops." Darrell stepped to the stable door and peered out through the crack. The name *Verrocchio* danced through her mind. Could it be?

Kate retreated into the darkness of the stall. "I'll wait in here," she said, her voice muffled by the wooden walls. "I'll sit here with Delaney and close my eyes.

If I try really hard, maybe I can convince myself this is all just a bad dream."

Darrell smiled and opened the door, suspended with leather hinges nailed tightly to the wooden wall of the stable. She glanced back and noted with satisfaction that she could see no sign of Kate in her hiding place. The old stable looked deserted, with only a few ramshackle stalls and a broken ladder leading to a tiny loft. She pulled the door inward and gave her eyes a moment to adjust to the brightness. Outside she could see a yard connecting the stable to a grand home, complete with a kitchen garden and pebble paths carefully lined with what looked like crushed clam shells.

We must be near the sea. Maybe there is *a cave we need to find after all.* Darrell hop-skipped her way into the kitchen garden. This leg was easier to walk on than the one she'd had in Scotland, but probably weighed double that of her prosthesis at home. She slipped under the spreading leaves of an olive tree and looked around.

This tree is almost as twisted as the arbutus at Eagle Glen. The thought gave her a pang as she brushed her hand along the gnarled trunk. She waited a full minute for anyone to appear, and then held her breath and scampered for a small doorway on the far side of the back wall, away from the kitchens.

The room was empty and almost as dark as the stable had been. A small fire burned low in a grate in one corner, providing the only source of light in the tightly shuttered room. Darrell stepped quietly around a table laden with parchment and other paper-like materials. She rubbed the oily texture of a page between her fingers.

A scratching sound under the far side of the table caused her to stop and peer through the gloom for any further sign of rodents. One rat was more than enough for the day. Rising onto the toes of her left foot, she cautiously stepped around the loaded table. The sound came again, and Darrell gathered her skirts around her knees and squinted at the surrounding floor.

Like a wraith rising from the ground, a ghostly white face hovered over the far side of the table. Darrell bit down hard on her lower lip to stop from yelling out loud.

"You're not going to scream, are you?" the head inquired.

Darrell, dumb with fear, shook her head.

"You can drop your skirts. There are no mice here, or rats either, for that matter. Dante looks after them." As if to prove the point, a cat slipped between her feet, arching his back against the chiselled wood of her leg. Thinking of Norton, her neighbour's cat, she reached down for a pat, but the cat slipped off into the shadows.

Darrell let the silky material of her heavy skirts rustle out of her numb fingers, and gathered her courage.

"You can't be a ghost," she said, somewhat unnecessarily, "though your face is so white, you look like one."

The pallid face took on a thoughtful expression as it examined Darrell. "How can you be so sure?" it asked, and then stood, removing all doubt.

Darrell, her initial fear gone, looked at the figure in front of her with some curiosity. She stepped around the table and gestured at the floor. "Most ghosts don't have feet."

"Perhaps then it is I who should worry about strange, spectral girls wandering about, as you clearly don't have feet either, from the sound of it."

Darrell flushed and sagged against the table for a moment, avoiding his eyes. Then she lifted her chin.

"You're right," she said quietly. "Though that does not make me a ghost, only a girl with one sound leg and one wooden."

"I knew it!" he exclaimed, and jumped at her in such a startling way she was forced to take a step backwards. "Let me see it, *per favore, per favore*! I want to examine how it works and how you are able to get around so well." Darrell stepped back again, amazed that someone taller than she could sound so much like a small boy wheedling for a treat.

"Certainly not!" She knew from her time in the fourteenth century that propriety would frown on her even being in this room unchaperoned with this young man, let alone showing him how her leg attached to the elaborate peg she wore under her heavy skirts. She frowned.

"How do you know I get around easily, anyway? Have you been spying on me?"

The young man looked abashed. "Not spying, really," he mumbled. "Just paying heed. I watched you walk in here and knew something to be amiss with your gait."

Her eyes adjusting to the gloom of the darkened room, Darrell took a good look at this curious non-ghost. She could now see his face appeared white because it was well-dusted with chalk, and his hair stood out from his head in tousled red ringlets, with chalk dust liberally distributed through it, as well. His hands were dirty and clutched a half-completed sketch along with the offending stick of chalk. From his appearance Darrell decided he must be fifteen or sixteen.

"You must be my friend's cousin."

Darrell raised her eyebrows, but didn't reply.

An impatient look crossed his face. "Well, are you or aren't you? Giovanni told me his cousin was coming to apprentice with my master for the season, but he didn't mention a girl."

"Oh? What *did* he say?"

"He said his cousin is coming here from afar, and will stay with his family." The young man gave her a long, appraising look, and then leaned over and lit a small taper from the fire in the corner grate.

Darrell frowned. "Did he say I am an artist, too?" she asked coldly.

"No, he did not. You are a girl, so I know it cannot be possible."

Darrell laughed, and the boy flushed bright red. "I am the one who should be laughing, not you. Girls cannot be artists!"

Darrell tucked her amusement into her cheek. "Why not?"

He looked flustered. "Well, because your job is to run the household, not to draw and paint. How can you sculpt or paint with any accuracy if you are not apprenticed to a professional artist? Besides," he scoffed, warming to his subject, "girls are stupid. They are not fit for a man's work. They cannot see the world through the eyes of humanity."

Darrell felt surprised at the extent of his prejudice. "Do you not think girls and women are human?" she asked.

He thought a moment. "I do believe they are human," he answered slowly, his eyes looking into the distance. "Just a little less human than men." He puffed his chest importantly, obviously proud of his membership in the superior gender of the species.

Darrell bit her tongue and changed the subject, sensing a lecture on women's rights might not find receptive ears at this moment. "What have you got there?" she asked, indicating the half-finished drawing.

He cast it carelessly down on the tabletop. "It is a study for an idea I have," he said, with a slight frown.

Darrell picked up the page. "It looks like a shield," she said. "Like a family emblem or coat of arms."

He looked at her with some admiration. "That is true. I am designing a crest to show my father — to show him..."

"To show him what?" Darrell was curious.

"To show him I can," he said, and slammed his hand on the tabletop. "I will show him all this and more. See here..." He pulled a small, leather-bound notebook from a satchel slung over a chair. "I write down all my thoughts and ideas and I keep them with me always." He flipped the pages, holding the book a little too close to her face.

Darrell stepped back. The book was half-filled with notes in some strange kind of code, drawings, art studies, and more.

"What is this?" she asked, sliding her finger into one of the pages.

A dark passion filled his eyes and he grinned ferociously. "This? This is the clock I designed to run with the power of water. And this? A study I made of birds that I will transform into a machine to make men fly — into the skies above us and perhaps one day into the past or the future."

Darrell jumped a little, her heart pounding at his words. She slipped over to the doorway. "I've got to go and find my friends," she murmured, fearful an adult would be drawn by the volume of his voice.

"I have to work anyhow," the young man sneered, having clearly forgotten his interest in her leg. "I don't have time to talk with stupid girls."

Darrell gritted her teeth. "I am not a stupid girl," she said. "My name is Darrell."

"Who cares for your ridiculous name?" he said, throwing back his shoulders. "After I complete this design, only one name in all of *Firenze* will be heard on everyone's lips."

Darrell lifted the corner of her own lip skeptically. "And that is?"

He grinned at her, and for a split second she was taken by the charm of his smile.

"Why, Leonardo, of course."

Darrell fled.

CHAPTER SIX

"You must be joking!" Brodie jumped up from his seat on an overturned wooden pail.

"No joke." Darrell paced around the small stall, lit now by the light of an oil lamp set precariously atop a bail of hay. "Besides, everyone knows Leonardo was apprenticed to Verrocchio."

Kate rolled her eyes. "Everyone? Sorry, Darrell, most people have trouble remembering all the major figures of the art world, let alone who their teachers were."

"Okay, okay. It's an interest of mine, that's all." Darrell held out her hands. "I *knew* his notebook looked familiar. And I touched the paper he was sketching on," she said in a whisper. "Do you know what that means to me?"

Brodie shook his head. "But why are we here? Is it to introduce Darrell to the greatest artist of all time? After our last visit, it seems a bit..."

"Shallow?" interjected Kate.

Darrell felt a splinter of anger deep in her chest. "What do you mean, shallow?" she said, her face hot. "It's not shallow to want to meet someone who changed the world — even if he is only a kid." She gestured angrily. "I wouldn't call you shallow if you wanted to meet the guy — ah, you know the computer guy..." She looked to Brodie for help. "Bill somebody..."

"Bill Gates?" Brodie guessed.

"That shows how much you know." Kate's face went as red as her hair. "Anyone who has any interest in technology knows that Gates has done more harm than good. He's a lucky idiot who was in the right place at the right time."

"All those computer guys are idiots. I'm just trying to make a point."

"Now, Darrell..." began Brodie.

"Stay out of this, Brodie," Darrell snapped.

"Are you calling me an idiot?" Kate snarled.

Darrell stuck her nose close to Kate's face. "My point, before you get all tied up in knots, is that you may want to meet the god of computers someday."

"Gates is *not* the god of computers," snarled Kate. "And who's getting worked up here?"

"Just a minute, Kate..." said Brodie, stepping to her side.

Both girls turned to Brodie. "Will you shut up?" they chorused.

There was a moment of complete silence...

...and Darrell laughed. "I'm sorry, Kate. I didn't mean to insult the computer god, whoever he is. Meeting

Leonardo da Vinci makes this the most amazing thing that has ever happened to me."

Kate chuckled, her anger clearly evaporated. "Okay, I get it. I didn't mean to insult Leonardo, either."

Brodie shook his head at the two girls. "I'm glad that's resolved. But if the purpose of this trip is for you to meet Leonardo, Darrell, then we should try to find our way back before Giovanni discovers I know more about fossils than I do about art."

"Fossils? What are these fossils, you speak of? And what are you saying about art?"

Darrell spun around. Their conversation had been so heated none of them had heard anyone enter the stable. And standing at the doorway was Giovanni, accompanied by a furious-looking man in clay-spattered clothes.

Darrell lay on a straw tick mattress across the room from Kate. A single candle burned low.

"I forgot how early they go to bed in these places," whispered Kate.

"Gives us a chance to talk," said Darrell. "And to figure out what to do next." She unwrapped the long strip of cloth that bound the uncomfortable wooden prosthesis to her leg with a sigh of relief. Tucking her sore leg beneath her, she shivered a little and pulled the rough woollen blanket close to ward off the chill. "Verrocchio was pretty angry at the idea that Brodie didn't want to improve his artistic skills."

"I think Brodie handled it really well. When he said

he was honoured to study under the great master, everyone cooled down pretty quickly."

"I stole one of the sheets of parchment from the table downstairs and a piece of chalk. As soon as it gets light in the morning, I'll do a quick sketch Brodie can pass off as his own. That should hold Verrocchio and Giovanni until we find a way to get out of here."

Kate sighed. "I wish we could spend more time drinking in the life here, instead of having to race to find a way out."

Darrell nodded. "Me, too. But until we know how to get home, I think we have to concentrate on finding the route back." She lay down, the straw in the pallet whispering beneath her. "What do you remember about getting here?"

"I remember walking down the stairs in the lighthouse, and then suddenly it felt like I was hauled through a tornado and kicked in the head.

"Yeah, I can relate." Darrell sat up. "The return journey must start from the small stable, Kate. We need to look through there tomorrow and see what we can find."

There was a puff of cool air and the tiny candle guttered and died. The door behind them creaked and a small, dark shadow crept into the room, panting. Darrell gasped and then felt a wet nose on her hand.

"Delaney! You scared us," she scolded, stroking him all the same. "And you smell a bit too much like stable," she added, wrapping her blanket around her shoulders. Delaney flopped to the floor beside her pallet and curled nose to tail. His presence comforted her, but even after the exhausting events of the day, it was a long time before sleep finally crept in and stole her thoughts away.

The girls awakened early, but were waylaid en route to the stable by the cheerful housekeeper. When they had been introduced to her the day before, she had exclaimed in delight at the sight of two extra pairs of hands to help with her labours.

"Even young ladies must learn the secrets of running a household," she had proclaimed. In the cool air of the new morning, Federica brought them to the kitchens, fed them a breakfast of a loaf of stale bread with a bowl of creamy milk to soften it, and put them to work. She chatted merrily the whole time but kept a stern eye on the assigned tasks. She shook her head and pursed her lips upon learning Kate's name.

"Katerina — and with red hair, too." She bent her head close to Darrell's. "You must carry the food into Leonardo for lunch today, Dara. He will throw the food in fury, otherwise."

"Why is that?"

Federica's smile was sad. "Leonardo's own mother was a maid, young as yourselves when she took up with his father. She came of poor stock, though, and even after the baby came he refused to marry her."

Kate's face flushed. "What do you mean, poor stock? You make it sound like she was one of the farm animals. And why is it only her fault about the baby?"

Federica clucked her tongue. "She showed little more wisdom than an animal, taking up with that man without benefit of the lord's blessing on the union." She reached over and patted Kate's arm kindly, softening her tone and leaving a trace of flour on Kate's freckled skin. "He has married another woman now, and Leonardo has legitimate brothers and sisters, heirs to their father's name."

"What happened to Leonardo's mother?" Kate prompted.

Federica shook her head disapprovingly. "The young maid Katerina — she found greener pastures and left Leonardo in care of his father."

"That is so sad," said Kate, and Federica nodded her agreement.

"Sad, yes, and I fear that it broke young Leonardo's heart. He will have nothing to do with women, as a rule, and it certainly will stir his emotions to find a flame-haired Katerina in the house."

"I'll stay right out of his way," promised Kate.

Darrell shrugged. "I've already met him, and your story explains a few things to me, Federica. I'll take his lunch in — though he'd probably be better off learning to get it himself."

Relief from their labours did not come until late morning, when Giovanni arrived, towing Brodie. Brodie grinned broadly at the sight of the two girls wrapped in aprons and dusty with flour.

"Now that we have completed our work soaking the clay, my grandfather has sent word that I am to bring these girls and my cousin Bruno to come before him," he told Federica, with a disdainful glance at Darrell and Kate. Puzzled, yet grateful for the reprieve, the girls slipped out of their aprons. Dusting flour off each other's skirts, they trailed behind the boys. The kitchens were actually made up of three separate rooms where different elements of food preparation were undertaken, and Darrell's face was bright red from working in the stifling room where the bread was baked in a wood stove. Kate had spent most of her time in the scullery, washing dishes in a large stone sink, before coming to help knead bread.

"Why do I always end up scrubbing things?" Kate whispered to Darrell.

"At least it wasn't floors," Darrell replied with a grin. She thought of Kate's red hands after her week as a scullery maid at Ainslie Castle, and she felt sure Kate remembered the experience just as vividly.

The large area behind the house held a number of small buildings, including the stable, enclosed by a high stone fence. Giovanni led them to a small structure, not much bigger than the stable.

"This is my grandfather's villa," he said in a formal tone. "He asked me to leave you here." He knocked sharply on the door twice and then swung it open. His eyes gleamed a vivid blue against the brown skin of his face. "Enjoy your conversation. My grandfather is anxious to meet you. And now," he said with a stiff nod, "I must return to my work." He walked off toward the main house, casting a curious glance over his shoulder before disappearing through the door.

They stepped inside and were ushered into a darkened room by an ancient woman as curled over as a comma and dressed entirely in black. It took a moment for Darrell's eyes to adjust from the brilliant day outside.

"I hope you don't mind the darkness. My old eyes don't enjoy the Tuscan sunlight any longer." The voice, resonant and low, drew them into the room. A man stood in one corner, leaning on an intricately carved wooden cane with a round, gold handle. He was not dressed in the same formal manner as the other men of the household, but wore black leggings, a simple white collarless shirt, and what looked like a grey travelling cloak flung over his shoulders.

"I'm so glad you found time to come," he said, and reached out to grasp Brodie by the hand. Striding to Kate without a trace of a limp, he swept her hand to his lips and smiled. "Keep courage, Katerina," he said quietly as she withdrew her hand and looked at him with puzzlement.

He turned to Darrell and she found her hand held fast in his cool, dry grasp. "Be seated," he commanded of Kate and Brodie without taking his eyes off Darrell. They sat obediently, side by side on a small, ornately embroidered sofa that was stuffed with some kind of coarse, straw-coloured hair that poked through the threadbare fabric. Darrell remained on her feet and stared curiously at the old man.

He smiled, but held Darrell's hand with an iron grip. "My name is Christofo Clemente and I am very pleased to make your acquaintance at last. Your leg must be terribly painful after standing all morning on that dreadful thing," he said softly, pointing his stick in the direction of the wooden prosthesis, completely hidden under her heavy skirts. "Please sit."

She nodded and perched on the edge of the chair he indicated. Her hands dropped into her lap, and she was aware only distantly that her fingers were suddenly cold after the heat of the kitchens. The old man slid into a chair that nestled behind a small desk in the corner.

The air felt heavy in the shuttered room and any noise from the rest of the household was muted and distant. Senor Clemente carefully propped his walking stick against the wall and placed both his hands flat on the desktop.

After what seemed like an hour of silence, he spoke. "Your time here will be very short, and we must make the best use of it we are able." He leaned forward with a secret smile. "I understand you go by the name Dara while you — visit — here?"

Darrell nodded again, wondering.

"I have reason to believe you may have a better understanding than I of what the future may hold," he said in a low voice. "But I have lived long years on this earth and I have learned much. Let us see what we may learn together, shall we?"

Darrell shook her head. "I — I don't understand."

His smile deepened. "You have had your future foretold before, young Dara?"

Darrell's thoughts flew to Luke and his Auntie Eileen in a time and place so far from this one. "Not really, sir," she managed to reply. "But..."

"Then you will not mind sharing your palm with me just this once?" he said, his voice resonant and low.

Darrell shot a look at Kate, whose expression showed her struggle between curiosity and the need to get away. Naturally, being Kate, curiosity won. She smiled her approval.

Brodie nodded from his seat, but his face was troubled and he leaned forward as though ready to leap at any moment to Darrell's rescue.

The old man reached over and with a flip of his hand cast open one of the mahogany shutters above his desk. A single beam of morning sun shot into the room, making Darrell's eyes water.

She looked down at her hands, now clasped loosely in her lap. In spite of the sunbeam, the temperature in the room seemed to drop, and she watched the hair on her arms rise and turn her skin to gooseflesh. For the first time, Darrell lifted her gaze and looked into his eyes. She felt a strange shock of recognition as pools of deep, clear blue looked back at her, without a sign of age or infirmity to be detected in their depths. Luke's eyes! Who was this man? And how could he share the eyes of a boy from another century?

"It is a matter of but a moment, my girl." He reached down and lifted her hand into the beam of mote-filled sunlight and turned her palm upward. With one finger he traced the blue veins pulsing at her wrist and then drew her fingers well back to better see her palm.

His smile faded. After less than a minute's scrutiny, he carefully folded her fingers over her palm and squeezed her hand.

"What did you see?" demanded Darrell.

His expression remained serious. He paused a moment and shook his head.

"What does it mean?" cried Kate. "Is it bad news?"

He chuckled and nodded kindly at Kate. "The palm doesn't give news, *mia cara*. It but gives pictures of possible futures, of things that might be."

"Or things that may not?" asked Darrell.

He met her steady gaze with his own. "You show a wisdom beyond your few years, *piccolina*," he said in a low voice. "And rather than paint pictures for you of what may or may not happen, let me tell you something your hand did not show me."

Darrell's mouth felt dry. "What do you mean?" she muttered.

Still holding her hand, the aged man bowed his head. His voice was the merest whisper.

"Hear me well. I know things with you are not as they would seem, and your time here is brief. Know this. Time does not forgive. It has no mercy. It befriends no one but death and is a twisted ally. When you dance with time, there is always a price to be paid."

He gazed pointedly down at the wooden peg supporting Darrell's leg. "Please God you have paid enough already." He grasped his cane and stood, and turned on his heel more nimbly than Darrell would have thought possible.

"I'd like you to have this, *mia cara*," he said, and placed the cane in Darrell's hands.

Darrell opened her mouth to decline but a glimpse of his eyes told her protests would be useless. "It's very beautiful," she whispered, gazing at the strange animals carved into the rich surface. "Thank you."

His hand was steady as he gestured toward the door. The tiny woman saw them out, her toothless mouth an empty moon of a smile.

As she reached the door, Darrell turned to look at the figure, still standing by his desk.

"Why did you want to see us if you could tell us so little?" she asked.

"An old man's indulgence," he answered, and his smile was sad. "It is important, when one is ready to move on, to know life will continue to flourish." He raised his hand in a mute gesture of farewell, and she never saw him again.

Leonardo's voice was the first thing Darrell heard as they stepped into the sunlit garden.

"Bruno, have you the sketch you promised Verrocchio?"

Brodie gave Darrell a quick wink. "It's right here," he said, pulling it out of his pocket with a flourish. "Sorry, it is a bit creased. I think Kate sat on it."

Leonardo reached to take the sketch but stopped with his hand in the air.

"Who sat on it?" he asked coldly.

Kate rolled her eyes. "I did not, Bro — Bruno." She looked at Leonardo. "He's teasing me," she explained.

Leonardo's lip curled and he turned his back on Kate to examine the sketch Darrell had drawn of the view from her window earlier that morning. Keeping his back to Kate, he spoke to Brodie. "You must come to show Verrocchio. He will be very pleased with your abilities."

Darrell spoke hastily, visions of Brodie's actual artistic ability in her mind. "He has promised to help us in *la cucina* until lunch."

"Help you in *la cucina*?" Leonardo laughed. "That is work fit only for women," he paused to glower at Kate, "and servants." He grabbed Brodie's arm. "Come with me now. I want you to show me how you make the *casa* in the background look so distant."

Brodie caught Darrell's frantic look. "I will follow you right away, Leonardo," he said. "But I have forgotten my chalk. I cannot draw without my own chalk."

"Very well then." Leonardo turned on his heel. "I will tell the master you are on your way."

"That was a close one," hissed Darrell as the door closed behind the young artist. "Look, Brodie, I think you need to suffer a serious hand-related injury right now. Your reputation as a great art student will go right downhill if they see how you really draw."

Brodie looked alarmed. "What do you mean by *serious*?" he asked.

Darrell laughed. "Wait here. I saw some rags in the kitchen that should do the trick." She ran into the kitchen, the walking stick making every step seem easier, and grabbed what she needed before the cook had time to turn around.

Darrell worked quickly on Brodie's hand. "Now don't forget. Federica told me everyone has a big lunch here and then a *riposino* in the hot hours of the afternoon."

"Okay." He nodded. "So while everyone is napping we can meet in the stable and look for the route back through to the lighthouse near Eagle Glen."

Kate nodded her agreement, and in moments Brodie's hand was bandaged with a rag, bloody from the remains of a chicken that had been slaughtered in preparation for the evening meal. His lip curling, Brodie headed inside to tell the master of his unfortunate accident with a kitchen knife.

"That was really gross." Kate chuckled.

"Gross, but as realistic as I could manage on short notice," said Darrell, dunking her bloody hands in a wooden bucket of water left beside the kitchen garden. "Hopefully they'll give him a job that will let him hide his true talent for now."

"*Ragazze!*" Federica's voice came bawling from the kitchen. "Girls! Where are you? I need you to help me with the *pranzo*."

Darrell shrugged. "It's only until after lunch," she promised Kate as they made their way back into the *cucina* to help prepare the midday meal.

"Federica tells me you want your lunch in here," Darrell said, as she set down a tray in front of Leonardo.

He grinned at her and smacked the table, making her jump a little. "Ha! Glad to see you doing the work you are meant for. Over here, beside me — and make it fast." Darrell's face burned. How could the artist who had produced so many beautiful things have been a young man like this? She moved the tray as requested and headed for the door, reminding herself that he didn't have the benefit of a twenty-first-century education.

She stepped over to the table and looked down at the sketches he had set to one side depicting a vicious-looking beast, fire leaping from its mouth.

"These sketches are wonderful," she admitted. "It looks like you have taken the body of a lion and added the head of a serpent, or perhaps a lizard."

"Yes, and the hind legs are actually those of a squirrel I found dead in the garden. I copied the shape of them and then lengthened them to resemble the legs of a horse," he responded, a note of pride in his voice. "This sketch is meant for the image on the shield I showed you earlier."

Leonardo walked around the table, his voice distant, as though lost in thought. "My father thinks he will get something any stupid farm boy could draw, but I will make him a masterpiece. Then we shall see what he thinks of the 'low arts,' as he calls them."

Darrell looked at him quizzically. "You sound so angry," she ventured. "But didn't your father arrange for you to learn art from Master Verrocchio?"

"Only for a year, until he can buy me a commission in the army. He thinks this is an easy way to keep me quiet and out of his hair." For the first time, Leonardo grinned, and he took Darrell roughly by the arm. "If you think these are good, wait until you see the finished result."

He whisked her over to a small closet and from the recesses drew out a large package wrapped in rough sacking. He pulled the sacking aside and Darrell gasped.

It was the beast from the sketches, painted in magnificent colour upon the surface of a shield.

"This will show him," Leonardo crowed. "He will see I am more than just a bastard son and know I am meant for more than life as a soldier or a notary."

Darrell nodded and headed for the door.

"Wait!" he barked, and she was forced to turn around. "What are you hiding?"

Darrell flushed. "What do you mean?"

He made an impatient move with his hands. "What are you hiding?" he repeated, and clarified, "In the stable."

"There are horses in the stable," she muttered, trying to sidle out of the room.

"Don't be stupid. There have been no horses in Verrocchio's small stable for years. What do you have in there that is not a horse?" He looked at her craftily. "You seem to be full of secrets, just like Giovanni's crazy grandfather. Perhaps I should take you back to him in his dark, foul *casa*. He would make you tell me."

"No — no. Don't do that." Darrell's thoughts raced. She didn't want anyone in the stable this afternoon, most particularly this arrogant young artist. "I'll tell you. It's my dog. I know he is not welcome in the *casa*, so I keep him out there."

"Oh." Leonardo looked disappointed and returned to his work, ignoring the lunch Darrell had brought.

"Aren't you going to eat?" she asked, as she turned to leave.

"I will eat as I have time. I must prepare these canvasses before this evening. If I do not finish in time, Master Verrocchio will have me flayed."

"Perhaps I could help you," Darrell offered, feeling a bit shy. "I have done a lot of canvas preparation in my time."

Leonardo looked shocked. "Certainly not!" he spluttered. "You are only a girl! Verrocchio would never allow it. Girls and women do not labour under his tutelage."

Darrell felt her temper flare.

"Well," she said, sarcasm dripping from every word, "I'm sure I couldn't possibly paint as well as any boy."

"You are mocking me," he said, his own face reddening. "No woman can paint with the talent of a man. Get back to your *cucina*, you *serva*."

Darrell stepped to the table and neatly overturned the entire contents of the lunch tray onto the freshly prepared canvas. "Enjoy your lunch, *Senor Porco*," she said sweetly, and then, clutching her new stick, hurried out of the room to the sound of his anguished roars.

Darrell hop-skipped her way into the kitchen and spied Kate right away, labouring over yet another pile of earthen crockery in the sink. "Where's Federica?" she hissed.

"She's gone to lie down," said Kate. "I was going to wait another minute or two and then come and find you. Shouldn't we be looking for the portal?"

Darrell could hear a roaring sound approaching from down the hall. "Something else has happened. We've got to go! Hopefully we can get to the stable and hide before…" She grabbed Kate's hand and pulled her out into the garden.

"Before what?" Kate, stumbling over the hem of her long skirt, yanked her arm out of Darrell's grasp and picked up her skirts in both hands. She dashed toward the stable. "Who's mad at you now, Darrell?" she called back over her shoulder, as Darrell hobbled behind.

"Never mind — I'll tell you later." Darrell closed the door and slid the latch. "Hopefully he won't think to look here."

"What's happening?" A voice from inside the stable made both girls jump. In her haste to bar the door, Darrell had missed the dim glow emerging from the stall where Kate had found refuge the previous day. The glow quickly coalesced around a small lamp held high as Brodie stepped out of his place in the stall, Delaney wagging at his side.

Darrell sighed in relief. "Look, Brodie, I don't have time to explain, but I don't think we can spend any time looking for the portal right now." She grabbed the lamp from his hand and looked around frantically. A partly broken ladder appeared in the circle of light, angling to a tiny loft above.

"That's going to have to be it." She was at the bottom of the ladder in an instant, peering up into the darkness of the loft. Angry voices swirled outside in the yard.

"Take this," she said firmly to Kate, handing her the lamp. She flung her stick into the loft and, pulling the ladder back as far as she could to lessen the angle, she patted the third rung. "Hop up, Delaney."

The dog put his front paws on the first broad rung and then ran to the top, nimbly hopping over a broken rung in the middle. He picked up Darrell's new walking stick and held it gently in his teeth.

"You next, Brodie."

"I'll go last," he said quietly. "I'm not afraid of these people."

"There's nothing to be afraid of," whispered Darrell. "I just want to stay out of the way for awhile — and I need you to pull me up this thing."

He rolled his eyes. "If you're hiding from someone, don't you think you should put out the light?" he said, as he scurried up to the loft.

"Oh yeah!" Darrell grabbed the lamp back from Kate and twisted the knob. The wick hissed out as Kate clambered to the top. She flipped easily onto her stomach and leaned over the edge of the loft beside Brodie. Darrell grabbed Brodie's arm and scrambled up, but missed her footing on the broken rung. She cried out as her left foot swung free, and the ladder slid to the stable floor with a thud. Four arms flailed in the darkness and managed to grab various parts of Darrell's anatomy and drag her over the edge.

"That was close," Kate breathed, still holding Darrell's hand. "Now are you going to tell us what happened?"

Darrell wiggled her skirt down to cover her knees, thankful the darkness hid her current deficiencies in the underwear department. "I had a bit of a problem with Leo..." she began. The door below them crashed open and light poured into the stable.

"I know she's in here somewhere," a furious voice thundered.

Darrell rolled onto her stomach and put her hand on Kate's arm, pulling her backwards. She reached her other hand out to Delaney, but at the touch of his fur she felt her hair blow straight back from her face as in the teeth of a winter storm. For an instant that seemed to last forever, she gazed down over the edge of the loft into the angry and astonished eyes of Leonardo. Then the wind took her and she was gone.

CHAPTER SEVEN

"You're kidding!" Kate's face was incredulous. "We got blasted back to the present because you had a *fight* with one of the greatest artists in the history of the world?"

Darrell felt sheepish. "Well — it was more of a disagreement than a fight," she said with mounting indignation, "and besides, I was right!"

She sat with Kate and Brodie in the deserted dining hall. It was early Saturday afternoon, and they had all recovered from the ordeal of the previous day. The night before, Darrell had found herself sprawled at the bottom of the spiral steps leading down from the lantern room, feeling like she had made it through the punishing final round of a wrestling bout. Nausea had coiled in her stomach like a sour serpent. Delaney licked her face twice and finally dropped an old stick on her chest before she was able to drag herself to her feet. Without thinking of anything but getting back to the school, she tucked the stick in her pocket and staggered off to find Kate and Brodie in the darkened lighthouse.

Dizzy and sick, they dragged themselves outside to find howling wind and driving rain. Darrell clutched Brodie's arm all the way back along the beach to avoid tripping over rocks in the raging night. By the time they reached the top of the path, sleet was stinging Darrell's eyes. They struggled in the front door only to face the wrath of Mrs. Follett for being out in such a storm. She bundled them all upstairs for showers. Fifteen minutes later, Darrell was staring at the clock in her room as she rubbed her freshly washed hair with a towel. It was six-thirty, and the whole adventure had apparently taken an hour and a half. Including the shower!

"It's strange that you wanted to hide in the stable," said Kate. "Didn't you realize it would be the first place that Leonardo would look?"

Darrell shrugged. "I wasn't thinking very clearly," she admitted. "I knew he would have to take the time to wipe his lunch off the canvases before they got stained, and I figured we would have a few minutes to decide what to do next if we hid in the stable."

"And instead, we got dragged forward through time." Kate looked thoughtful.

"I think we need to look at this thing scientifically," said Brodie. "Last summer when we travelled through the cave, Darrell touched the glyphs on the wall." He paused. "But this time — no cave, no glyphs. Just the lighthouse."

Kate shivered. "It's so weird to think we have some kind of portal to the past right down the beach from where we're sitting now. I mean, anybody could go through it."

"I don't think that's true," said Brodie. "If that was the case, everyone who has ever worked in the lighthouse could have been flipping back and forth through history. And what about the people who use the old hayloft in the stable? Do you see them dropping by for a visit?" He looked at Kate. "No. Think about it — who travelled through the cave?"

"Well, duh! We all did."

Brodie turned his eyes to Darrell. "No," he said, "that's not quite right."

"I did," she whispered. "With Delaney. Every time. If you guys were touching me, you came, too."

Brodie nodded. "So, if conditions are right, we can all travel through as long as we have Darrell and Delaney."

"But the cave had those three glyphs," said Kate. "Somehow they helped move us through time. What made it work in the lighthouse?"

Brodie shook his head. "I don't know. But I'd like to go back and run a little test."

Kate stiffened. "Oh no — I don't think I'm ready yet, Brodie. I mean — I love this time travel thing, it's really interesting and everything, but — I'm just not ready to head back yet. What if we got turned around and went into the future instead?"

Darrell jumped in her chair, feeling as though a tiny shock had crackled along her spine. She opened her mouth to speak, closed it, and gave her head a little shake.

Brodie crumpled the paper napkin under his elbow and tossed it at Kate. "You goof! I didn't mean we should take another trip into the past. As a matter of fact, I want to be completely safe, so I think Darrell and Delaney shouldn't come at all."

Kate flipped the napkin back. "In that case, I don't think I need to be there either." She shuddered. "I don't want to go near the lighthouse for a while. My stomach needs a chance to settle for a few days."

Brodie shrugged. "Okay by me. Still, it's best to have an independent observer in any experiment. How about if you stay outside and watch from a distance? That way you can let Darrell know if I disappear and she has to come and find me."

He laughed at Kate's look of horror. "I'm kidding! You can be the lookout to make sure no one comes along while I'm checking the place out. It'll only take me five minutes or so."

Kate turned to Darrell, who sat in her chair fiddling with the old bit of stick she had taken from Delaney. "You seem awfully quiet about this," Kate said. "Do you think it's safe for Brodie to go back into the lighthouse?"

Darrell gave a little start. "What?" She looked at her friends' expectant faces and tried to remember what they had been talking about. "The lighthouse? Sure. Do you want me to come?"

"Have you heard a word we've been saying?" asked Kate. She raised her eyebrows at Darrell and turned back to Brodie. "Okay, I'll come, as long as we keep the space cadet here as far away as possible."

Brodie jumped to his feet, but Kate stood more slowly, staring at the solid wall of rain outside the window, her face a mask of gloom. "I need to go find an umbrella first," she said, "although I don't know why I bother. That rain is going straight sideways."

Darrell waved absently as they left, but stayed in her seat, staring into the empty expanse of the dining hall. She slipped Delaney's old stick from her pocket, tracing her fingers over lines so thin as to be barely visible, and remembered the last look of anger and puzzlement she had seen in Leonardo's eyes.

After examining the fine markings on the old stick for an hour, Darrell came to a decision. She spent the afternoon in the school library, poring over books about a certain genius artist of the Renaissance era. Delaney curled contentedly under her chair as Darrell devoured everything she could find on the subject. At dinner, Brodie and Kate related their experience of spending what turned out to be the entire afternoon running up and down the stairs in the lighthouse, and they talked about it in what seemed like endlessly tedious detail. At the end of the meal, Professor Myrtle Tooth stood and announced the schedule for mid-term exams, slated to begin the following week and run until Thanksgiving weekend.

Everyone groaned and Kate slapped her forehead. "Argh! Tests in math and computers won't be so bad, but I am so dead in English and history."

Brodie chuckled. "Since Professor Tooth usually gives essay questions, I think you may be able to find something to write about the Renaissance, don't you?"

Kate's face brightened. "Right!" She reached over and poked Darrell with a pencil. "That won't be so bad, will it?"

Darrell smiled automatically. "Yeah, not so bad."

Kate grabbed Darrell's shoulder and shook it a little. "What are you thinking about? You haven't eaten anything and I don't think you've said more than a few words in the past hour."

Darrell stood and slid her chair back into place at the table. "I'm not very hungry, that's all. I'll see you guys later. I've got to go study." She stuck her books under one arm, grabbed her tray with the other hand, and left the table, hardly noticing the puzzled glance exchanged by Kate and Brodie.

Over the course of the next week, Darrell spent most of her spare time in the library. She even gave up time in the art room to spend reading and making notes about Leonardo's life. She read how he professed to have no use for women and how his mother had been a servant girl named Katerina with whom he had little or no relationship. *Federica was right. A mother who abandoned him and a father who paid little attention. No wonder he was so rude.*

However, much of what she found in the library proved unsatisfactory, and it irritated her to see how often the authors of history textbooks were wrong about the simplest details of everyday life. She read about the china dishes used in Italian kitchens and scoffed, remembering Kate's busy morning labouring over sinks full of pottery

and earthenware and the endless stream of wooden platters they had to wash after the evening meal. She even
laughed a little when reading about the elaborate underwear said to be worn by the nobility of fifteenth-century
Florence. But for the most part she felt just one emotion.

Frustration.

Frustration that there was so little available about
the man who interested her most. She read tedious
tomes about the history of the period, and the Medici
family who sponsored many wonderful artists of the
era, including Leonardo for a time. But she couldn't
find a single source of information written by someone
who knew Leonardo. Really knew him — knew how he
spent his days, knew his low regard for girls and
women, knew his passion for his art and what his deepest thoughts revealed.

When she ran out of resources in the library, Darrell
turned to the Internet. She didn't want to share her
ideas with Kate, so she used the school computers to
find out more. Initially, she was thrilled to discover
more information about Leonardo's notebooks on-line,
but the euphoria of this discovery was dashed when she
examined the collections and found many had been cut
up or lost by his friends and heirs.

*I know he wrote about time travel. He told me he was
going to invent a machine to travel through time. It must
be here somewhere!*

Kate and Brodie were immersed in their own studying but still teased Darrell, saying they never saw her anymore. It was true — she had stopped going to the study
room altogether, instead spending all her time in the

library or the computer lab, poring over documents. Twice she had to be summoned to write an exam, and on the Friday before Thanksgiving weekend, she only just managed to turn her art portfolio in to Mr. Gill on time.

"Haven't seen much of you in the studio lately," he remarked, as she handed him the folder, its cover still damp and redolent of fresh ink. "Been studying for exams?"

Darrell nodded. "I've — been a bit too busy for art, I guess," she said, averting her eyes.

Mr. Gill frowned. "Don't bury yourself so deeply in your studies that you can't find time for your art, Darrell," he said, his voice stern. "It's a huge part of who you are."

Darrell had nodded mutely and left the room. But she thought about the conversation later that night as she lay, feeling like a stranger in her own bed at home in Vancouver, staring unseeing at the ceiling.

A huge part of who I am. The memory left her heart bleak. *And just who am I? A kid with one leg. A kid with no dad. A kid who likes art, but who cares about that? It's only a way to forget about my leg and my dad.*

And as the autumn moon rose to cast its thin glow across her bed, she caressed the idea that had been driving her since her return from Florence. She looked down at the bulge her left foot made under the covers and the flat expanse of bedclothes where her right foot should be. *What if he did find a way to make a time machine? What if it was among the lost papers? I know where he kept his notebooks — he showed me. I know he wanted to discover the secret of time.*

From her end table, she picked up the stick Delaney had dropped on her as she lay on the floor of the light-house. The intricate carvings were long lost, though thin lines still traced across its worn and dirty surface. Still, there was no doubt in her mind. She knew it for what it once was. For the first time, she had brought something home with her, even if it no longer resembled the beautifully carved walking stick it once had been.

She sat up in bed, no longer seeing her legs, or the covers, or the silver moonlight. All she could see were eyes from another time. Leonardo's eyes, staring at her — thinking about her — as she disappeared through a hole in time.

She had to go back to find out just how much he knew.

The next morning began her first full day home for the long weekend, but Darrell waved off her mother's offer of a shopping trip and caught the bus to the main branch of the Vancouver Public Library. Faced with the size of the Renaissance section, her head reeled. This one section dwarfed the entire library at Eagle Glen.

I've got to start somewhere. She pulled out the first book in the stacks.

Ducking her mother's suggested activities, Darrell spent every day of the long weekend at the library. Her list of questions was so long she soon learned the name of every research librarian who was on shift when she appeared each day. Her best find was an old, leather-bound tome depicting both images and text from a few of Leonardo's manuscripts.

The manuscripts were fascinating. Darrell read through reams of reproductions of Leonardo's work, held in collections from Milan to Britain to Paris. She even read, with some amusement, that Kate's nemesis, Bill Gates, was the only known private collector to possess one of Leonardo's manuscripts.

Studies of horses, mechanics, and geometry competed with long lists of notes on the subject of wind and water currents. Darrell saw a fragment of a sketch of a bird in flight that gave her a jolt of recognition and read that it had been taken from a diary of Leonardo's circa 1471. Confirming in her notes that he was born in 1452, Darrell realized she had met Leonardo when he was around nineteen years old, a mere two years before fame would begin to swirl about him and wrap him in its golden cape.

Though Leonardo's journals were well known for their strange mirror writing, Darrell realized she could read none of the Italian script, apart from the famous signature. Remembering her fluency in Italian while on the journey, she filed this information away for later use. If she did manage to find the secret to Leonardo's time machine, she would need to try to copy it down in English so she could put it into use more readily when she got back to the school.

Janice Connor drove in silence, and Darrell stared out the window, trying to ignore her mother's sideways glances. A whole weekend in the library and she still had so much to learn.

"You've been so quiet this weekend, Darrell. Are you tired?"

Darrell's head jerked up, startled. "Oh — yeah — I guess so." She coloured a little. "My mid-terms were quite hard, and I'm — well, I'm working on an important project, and it's been keeping me really busy." She smiled at her mother. "So, yeah, I guess I am pretty tired."

Delaney stirred in the back seat and rested his chin on the door. He gazed out the window with half-closed eyes, dozing.

Janice laughed, catching sight of the dog in the rear view mirror. "I guess you're not the only one who's tired. But try not to overdo it, okay?"

Darrell smiled and reached back to give Delaney a pat. His tail thumped in response.

"He's just recovering from a weekend with Norton," Darrell said, with a grin.

Her mother nodded. "That cat keeps him pretty busy." Delaney swished his tail and settled further into his spot on the back seat.

The rain lashed the windshield as they drove out of the city, but by the time they reached the highway it petered out and the sun began to break through the morning clouds.

"It's good to get away from all the noise in the city," remarked Darrell. "I forget what it's like when I've been at school for a while."

She leaned her head on the side window and wondered about fall in Italy. Would they have had snow or would it be wet, like here? She compared this past weekend in the city, where thousands of people bustled along the crowded streets under multicoloured umbrellas, with her memory of houses lit by candles and oil lamps. She laughed aloud.

"What's so funny?"

"Nothing. I guess I was thinking about how Vancouver is so different from anywhere else."

Janice shot Darrell a quick glance as she drove down the nearly deserted highway. "You spent almost the whole weekend in the library. What's this big project you're working on?"

Darrell shrugged and turned a little pink. "Just — some stuff for the Renaissance fair we're having before Christmas. We've got to make it as authentic as possible, and I needed to look up some stuff on the Renaissance."

Darrell's mother nodded. "I guess I'm more used to seeing you spend all your time with your head in a sketchbook."

"Well, I still worked on my art a little. But I needed some fresh research material for this project I'm working on, that's all."

Janice pulled into the long school driveway. "It's okay by me, sweetheart." She glanced over at her daughter, speculation in her eyes. "Eagle Glen has changed you, y'know," she said, her voice soft.

Darrell stiffened. "What do you mean?"

Her mother smiled. "I'm not sure. Some of your anger seems to be gone. But I can't put my finger on what's replaced it." She drummed her fingers on the wheel. "Determination? Focus? I don't know."

Darrell laughed, but her voice sounded hollow. "I don't know either, Mom." She stared out her window at the bare cherry trees and the waning maples. The long weekend had flown by. Her mother had taken a day off to celebrate Thanksgiving by cooking an enormous turkey. But Darrell had spent the whole weekend formulating her plans, which gnawed at her like a tickertape running along the base of her brain.

What would her mother think if she found a way to change the past? Darrell stared out the window, imagining the look on her mother's face when she walked in the front door on two sound legs. Or even better, if she got carried in on the back of her wonderful, beautiful, perfect father, as if the accident had never happened. Okay — so her mom hadn't believed her father was wonderful or perfect. They were divorced, after all. But maybe Darrell could find a way to fix that, too.

"Thanks for bringing us back early, Mom." Darrell flung her arms around her mother's neck as they stood near the front door of Eagle Glen. Delaney jumped out of the car and took off around the back of the school, his nose to the ground. "I can get a head start on my project, now."

"Well, it worked better for me, too," said her mother, hugging back. "I have surgery scheduled this afternoon and this gives me a chance to get back and do my rounds beforehand. Love you!" She kissed her daughter's cheek, and with a wave to Mrs. Follett in her spot at the front door, she drove off in a spray of gravel.

Darrell had a quick look around for Delaney, but he was nowhere to be found.

"Back in his old hunting ground," she muttered, smiling a little. She gathered up her suitcase and backpack and headed into the school. To her disappointed surprise, standing in the shadows behind Mrs. Follett at the door was Conrad Kennedy.

"Isn't this nice, dear? You can be good company for Conrad, since he's here as well."

"I don't need company," snarled Conrad and turned on his heel.

"Now, dear, don't be like that," Mrs. Follett called after him, but he disappeared in the direction of the music room.

"I'm sorry, dear," Mrs. Follett twittered at Darrell. "I'm afraid Conrad wasn't very happy at having to spend the long weekend at the school."

"He didn't go home?" Darrell said in surprise. "Wasn't the whole school shut down?"

"Oh no, dear. The buildings remain open and a few of the staff stay as well." She leaned towards Darrell conspiratorially. "I'm on my own since Mr. Follett passed on, God rest his soul, and since we still can't seem to get a hold of Conrad's mother, I was hoping he would agree to come home with me. In the end, he decided to stay at the school with the custodian and Mr. Gill."

For a moment, Darrell felt a little pity for a boy whose mother couldn't be troubled to bring him home for Thanksgiving, but as the discordant sounds of an amplified guitar turned up high came pounding out of the music room, she changed her mind.

Once a creep, always a creep. After assuring Mrs. Follett that no, she didn't require a second breakfast, Darrell strode up the stairs of the school.

Filled with nervous excitement, she flung her backpack on her bed and began to make the preparations for her journey. Every time she had journeyed through the fabric of time, whether to ancient Scotland or to Renaissance Italy, one thing stood out. Somehow, in a way she could not begin to understand, time seemed to compress in the past. Journeys that seemed to last days turned out to have taken only a few minutes. She felt certain her absence on a trip of any length at all would not be noticed, and if things went according to plan, she was hoping to be in and out of Verrocchio's home in a matter of minutes.

A loud crash resonated from somewhere in front of the school. Darrell fumbled several of the items she was loading in her pocket and they dropped to the floor. She scooped up a tiny notebook, a roll of mints, a large pad of soft cotton, and her fragment of stick and jammed them into her pockets. She ran out of her room and down the hall until she found a classroom with windows fronting the school building. It was surprising to discover the noise wasn't the result of Conrad smashing a guitar to bits on the front lawn or making any disturbance at all. Instead, she saw a huge flatbed truck idling at the front of the school, with several other trucks pulling in the driveway. The truck had just unloaded a small construction Caterpillar down a metal ramp, and that must have been the source of the crash.

Torn, Darrell hesitated. Should she look into what was going on with this equipment or make her way down to the beach? After a moment's indecision, she decided this was too great a diversion not to take advantage of. A quick peek over the banisters confirmed Mrs. Follett was busy talking to the driver of the Cat, and Darrell slipped down the back stairs and out the side door near the kitchen.

Delaney came bolting around the corner as more equipment crashed at the front of the school, and Darrell rubbed his ears to calm him down.

"Let's go for a walk, boy," she whispered and headed down the path to the beach. The sky was a watery blue, and a thin winter sun pushed its way through the wisps of cloud. A stiff breeze was blowing off the ocean, though it eased somewhat when Darrell emerged from the path at the base of the cliffs.

She paused to catch her breath and then scurried to find a place to hide behind one of the large boulders at the bottom. A few large rolls of industrial fencing lay on their sides nearby, and as she watched, a small Caterpillar similar to the one in front of the school scooped up a roll and trundled off down the beach. It looked like the lighthouse demolition had begun. Darrell smacked her forehead with the palm of her hand and sat down behind the boulder to think up a solution to this new problem.

A whistle shrieked and Delaney jumped at the sound. Darrell was huddled with her back against a rock, alternately feeling frustration because of the delay and gratitude for the thin sunshine. A wait like this in the rain would have been torture.

Luckily, I'll only need a few minutes. She stroked Delaney's back to calm him. *Besides, this demolition project will probably take weeks to complete.* While she watched, a pair of construction workers began to unroll the fencing around the lighthouse, but at the sound of the whistle, the small Caterpillar turned a tight circle and drove straight for Darrell's hiding place.

I'm only watching the workers. I was bored and thought I'd sit here and watch.

Excuse formulated, she wrapped her arm around Delaney's neck and waited. The Cat lurched to a halt on the other side of Darrell's boulder, and she heard the crunch of gravel as the workers jumped out and marched up the pathway. She looked up, but they walked right by her, silver Thermoses in hand.

The power of coffee. She grinned with satisfaction. *I love living on the West Coast.*

She gave the men to the count of one hundred to labour up the path in their heavy construction boots, then slipped out from behind the boulder, Delaney at her heel. Keeping close to the cliff, she hop-skipped her way over the protruding stones on the firm sand of the beach. Where the rock wall curved to meet the lapping waves, she paused and gazed back toward the path and the school. Nothing. Not even a seabird hopping along the shore. No one could see her and nothing stood in her way.

Her heart gave a sudden lurch and she stumbled, trying to find her footing on the rocks at the base of the lighthouse. "Come on, Delaney. Let's go find that arrogant artist."

She stepped easily over the uninstalled fencing lying loose on the ground and, Delaney in the lead, slipped under the chain barring the door.

CHAPTER EIGHT

Tiny specks of dust and wisps of straw floated in the sunbeam pouring through a crack in the wall of the small stable, and Darrell decided to finish the mint she had popped in her mouth before moving again. She'd already clonked her head on the walking stick, and the egg-shaped bump above her hairline convinced her to slow down a little. Lifting her arm gingerly, she held the ornate stick in the sunbeam, marvelling. The round gold handle seemed a little loose, but that had probably been caused by her own hard head. She thrilled at the feel of the stick in her hands, returned to its former glory. A glow of triumph warmed her and she sat up, bumped head forgotten.

Her theory was right! Delaney had picked up the walking stick in his teeth the last time they were in this stable. The stick he dropped on her in the dark of the lighthouse had looked like a broken piece of drift-wood, but...

What would have happened if she hadn't stuffed it in her pocket? It wasn't until the next day when she went to throw it away that she noticed the fine lines in the wood, carved by an artisan long dead.

She rolled the ornate stick between her fingers. The wood was a rich mahogany colour and the bottom of the stick looked well worn. *I don't remember noticing that before.* Not that there had been time for noticing much of anything.

"And there's no time to waste right now, either," she whispered to Delaney. She pulled up the hem of her heavy brocade overskirt and unwrapped the long cloth that bound the wooden peg into place. Darrell swiftly folded more soft padding into the hollow opening at the top of the carved wooden prosthesis. It was a matter of less than a moment more to replace the wooden leg below her right knee and rewrap it securely in place. Creeping along so as not to put too much weight on the knee, she peered over the edge of the tiny loft and nearly jumped out of her skin as a pony whickered in the stall below. Delaney brushed past her and lightly tiptoed down a rickety set of steps.

These are new. The wooden steps didn't look new, but Darrell remembered the broken ladder they had all struggled up on the last trip. As there was no handrail, it seemed easiest to turn around and hop down the steps on her left foot. A broken riser in the middle proved to be a little tricky, but she managed it and got down at last. She peeked around the corner at the small pony tethered in the stall. Placidly chewing on a wisp of hay, he lifted his head and gazed calmly at her a moment before ducking back for another bite.

She turned to Delaney. "Stay!" she said in as stern a voice as she could muster, and the dog dropped to the straw-covered floor of the stable, paws curled under. He looked up at her and raised alternating eyebrows.

"Good boy. I should be back in a few minutes."

Darrell clutched her walking stick, grateful for its support, and poked her head out of the stable door. The yard appeared to be empty. The sun shone down from almost straight overhead, and the air was still and hot. An insect thrummed, and Darrell noted with satisfaction that all movement seemed to have slowed down, as people slept through the warmest part of the day. A trickle of sweat slipped down her spine, and she crept along the path a few steps before realizing something was missing.

The kitchen garden sat still and green in the autumn sunshine, but the wall behind it was new, made of stone fitted neatly together, mortarless. Where was Cristofo's tiny villa? Fruit trees heavy with ripe pears formed a small orchard where the villa had stood within the stone walls of the yard.

A sliver of doubt wedged painfully into the back of Darrell's brain. She made her way to the kitchen door.

"Federica?" The girl shook her head. "I'm sorry, *signorina*. Are you sure you have the correct villa?"

Darrell nodded, her frustration growing. "It doesn't matter. I haven't been to visit Verrocchio for a while," she said, trying to curb her impatience, "and I just need to find his student, Leonardo. Can you show me to his room?"

The maid tucked a strand of hair into her kerchief. "Master Leonardo has not lived here since he was a boy. His studio is close to the centre of the city." She eyed Darrell with growing suspicion. "Everyone knows this. What did you say your name is?"

Realization hit Darrell so hard she practically heard her brain click. "My name is Dara. I — I come from..." She searched her mind and settled on the home city of her mother's grandparents. "Verona. I have only this afternoon to visit my father's friend Leonardo. Can you direct me to his home?"

Slightly mollified, the maid pointed Darrell in the direction of the studio, apparently not too far away. Darrell headed off down the lane. A last look over her shoulder showed the maid still standing outside the door in Verrocchio's yard, a frown on her face and hands on her hips.

Darrell slipped around a corner in the lane and then stopped to think a moment. Time had passed, of course. The small villa behind the main house was gone. Giovanni's grandfather, Cristofo, was probably gone, too, long dead and buried.

Her heart sank at the thought of those piercing blue eyes, now finally stilled forever. The walking stick was worn down and the ladder in the stable had been replaced with a set of steps. She should have noticed these changes. But how much time had passed? A cool nose pressed against her leg and she started.

"Delaney! I thought I told you to stay!" Instead of impatience, sudden relief flooded through her, and she bent over to rub his ears.

"You'll help me find him, won't you, boy?"

But even with Delaney at her side, her luck didn't improve. The directions given by Verrocchio's maid seemed clear enough, but Darrell was soon so turned around by the maze of lanes and streets that it wasn't long before she realized she was lost. She hurried from one street to the next, looking for the low, white building with a marble lion guarding the doorway that Verrocchio's maid had described. She followed the winding streets, twisting one moment along a lane lined with row houses hunched and dark like crows on a line and then, steps away, broadening into a *piazza* lined with beautiful buildings or the elegant arches of a stone *loggia*.

Florence came alive as the warmth of the day gave way to the cooler air of evening. Darrell felt nearly frantic with worry. Her leg throbbed in spite of the soft cotton pad she had applied under the prosthesis. A red blister had risen on the palm of her left hand from her over-enthusiastic use of the walking stick. She had spent most of the afternoon trying to find her way through the humid streets of Florence, and now found herself wandering down a treeless lane without a clue as to where she was.

The unmistakeable aroma of the river rose in the cooling air. Earlier, Darrell had crossed the Arno on a tiny footbridge but now decided to return across a strange bridge she spied that embraced the shallow river. She stepped carefully along a narrow cobbled path that threaded its way across the bridge. The bridge contained a number of strange edifices of different sizes and shapes. Butchers jostled with merchants, and shops abutted tiny apartments where people seemed to live, all atop the slender bridge crossing the river. The bridge was teeming with people.

As a small child ran shrieking by, Darrell clutched at his arm. He shrank against a wall as if he expected to be struck. "Excuse me," said Darrell, her voice quiet among the cacophony on the bridge.

The boy eyed her warily. "I didn't steal it — it was m' bruther."

Darrell gave him a tired smile. "Don't worry. I'm only trying to learn the name of this bridge."

A huge smile spread across his face, revealing all four front teeth missing. "*Ponte Vecchio*," he replied promptly, adding, "I thought you was after me for the apple I took from the basket back there."

Darrell released his grimy sleeve and her smile broadened. "Wasn't it your brother who took the apple?"

"Yeah, well it was for him that I took it." He pointed to his gaping mouth. "Can't chew!" He dashed away, giving her a final impish grin over one shoulder.

Darrell laughed out loud, but immediately regretted it. Many of the merchants on the *Ponte Vecchio* were butchers, and they threw the offal from recently slaughtered animals and birds right into the river. This, Darrell thought, holding an almost completely useless lace handkerchief to her nose, probably accounted for the smell. How could a city so sumptuous in architecture smell so bad?

She hurried between the tiny shops and homes on the bridge and was soon across. The streets were beginning to empty, and a chill settled in the air. Though not the cool, rainy fall that she was used to, it was obviously autumn here in Florence, as well. Many trees were heavy with fruit and leaves were beginning to fall, making the ground treacherous for a girl balancing on a wooden leg.

The sun seemed to fall out of the sky and it became dark. Darrell's stomach rumbled and she felt ready to drop from exhaustion. Apart from the Arno behind her, she could not see a single familiar landmark. She stopped to rest on the wide, marble rim of a small fountain. Splashing water on her face made her feel better, though her stomach roared with hunger.

"We'd better find something to eat, Delaney," she began, and then realized Delaney was no longer at her side. She looked up the street to see that he stood at the entrance to a small park. In the distance, Darrell could hear the notes of a stringed instrument, as though it were being tuned.

"Delaney!"

He barked once and stood his ground, tail wagging. Darrell got up and walked wearily over to the dog. As she neared him he barked again and dashed into the gated park. Muttering to herself about poorly trained dogs who wouldn't come when called, Darrell stepped in through the gate. As she entered the small park, the music she had heard while by the fountain swelled around her, and Delaney loped over and capered at her feet in a most undignified manner.

"Come on, Delaney, we've got to get —" Someone jostled her from behind, and in her tired state she nearly fell. Delaney dashed off again and Darrell felt her arm suddenly grasped.

"*Grazia*," she said to the man who held her up.

"Your pardon, *signorina*. My fault entirely." Even in the failing light, Darrell could see his face was red, and he held a large flagon of wine. "A torch!" he cried. "Light the torches! The sky darkens and I call for light!" Flames flared throughout the small park as candles were put to pitch and Darrell looked around with amazement to find she was in the midst of a celebration.

The park was larger than she had first thought, for its private entrance had been through a bower of low shrubbery, but inside it opened to a wider expanse, tree-lined and lush. A long swath of fabric had been draped over the branches and a few wooden posts along one side of the open area. Under this makeshift tent was a huge trestle table loaded with food.

Party guests were divided among those who milled around the table collecting food and those who had abandoned empty plates and had turned to dancing. Someone grasped her hand, and Darrell was pulled into an energetic group who spun and swirled and stomped the ground until it shook.

"I'm sorry," she gasped to her partner, a girl who appeared to be a few years her junior, "I don't know this dance." The girl smiled and twirled off, and Darrell had to step quickly to extricate herself without injury from the enthusiastic group. The music was played by a versatile foursome who, judging from the variety scattered nearby, played at least fifteen or twenty instruments between them.

"The bride!" "The groom!" A landau swung into view, bearing a young couple who laughed and held on for dear life. They were paraded into the clearing on the shoulders of four strong young men, to the cheers of well-wishers in the party. The landau was set down with much fanfare, and the bride and groom got unsteadily to their feet. The bride wore a gown of vivid red silk, with slashes cut in the arms and skirt to reveal a heavy blue brocade. Tied around her waist was a small cloth bag that well-wishers filled with gold coins as she was whirled through the crowd. The groom, dressed equally colourfully, was spun off in another direction. Darrell smiled, wondering if the man who had bumped into her was the proud father of the pretty young girl who could not help laughing as she was twirled from one partner to the next.

"*Ne di Venere Ne di Marte non si sposa ne si parte!*" A tiny woman dressed fully in black with a glittering gold shawl over her shoulders shook a thick finger under Darrell's nose. "Neither marriage nor war will go away once you start," she repeated, and her eyes twinkled as she pointed the same finger toward the food.

Darrell stepped nearer to the makeshift tent, drawn by the warmth and the smell of the food, and had a large clay plate thrust into her hands.

"Eat!" commanded the small woman. Darrell was relieved to hear that the woman seemed to greet everyone who approached the table with the same tone, and gratefully stepped forward to make her selection. Saliva flooded her mouth at the sight and smell of enormous pots of rich beef stew, roasted chickens skewered and decorated with apples and plums, and what appeared to be a large tart made with onions and sausage.

Signs of a fruitful fall harvest were everywhere. Baskets of peaches dotted the table, and a large barrel entirely filled with grapes of many colours sat on the ground. Wooden platters loaded with cheese and bread were being continually replenished by a gleeful group of girls who all looked to be under ten years old.

Darrell set her loaded plate down and sat gratefully at a nearby table. She reached under the elaborately embroidered cloth to feed Delaney a piece of chicken from her plate, but it was snatched from her fingers by another dog. She looked around but couldn't see Delaney anywhere. *Guess he'll have to look after himself.* She turned ravenously to her meal. A large bonfire had been lit on one side of the park, and as she ate, Darrell watched small children run and dance around it, vibrant silhouettes against the flames.

Her stomach full, and her sore leg somewhat rested, Darrell wandered through the celebration in search of Delaney. Dogs ran to and fro with the children, and by this time the party numbered in the hundreds as neighbours and friends greeted each other with shouts and effusive rituals involving much bowing and kissing. Darrell smiled at the elaborate display and sat down on a pile of straw near the fire to wait for Delaney.

I'll just warm up for a moment and then I'll ask someone for directions back to Verrocchio's home. And this time I'll write them down.

CHAPTER NINE

It was the creeping cold that first made Darrell aware
things were not as they should be. It pushed into her
brain by way of the toes on her left foot and the fingers
of both hands. She awoke with a start in the first light
of dawn to find Delaney once more curled at her side,
the fire out, and a group of old women in black chattering merrily as they gathered the dishes and cleaned
up after the feast.

With a sinking heart, Darrell realized she had slept
the night through. She struggled to stand and discovered someone had wrapped her in a heavy woollen
cloak as she slept. Delaney was slow to rise, and as he
stood, Darrell noticed he was covered in mud.

"What have *you* been into?" she whispered, as
Delaney thumped his tail on the ground and yawned cavernously. She limped over to where the grandmothers
bobbed like old crows as they tidied away the remains of
the feast.

"Sleep well?"

Startled, Darrell looked into the twinkling eyes of the old woman in the gold shawl who had commanded her to eat the night before. She nodded and the woman took the cloak from Darrell and folded it away with a practiced hand.

On impulse Darrell spoke. "I need to find the studio of the artist Leonardo. Do you know where it is?"

The old one nodded and smiled, showing bright pink gums home to a single yellow tooth. She pointed up the street behind the small park. "Up that way, young woman. A low, white building. Look for the stone lion." She pursed her lips. "Surely you do not travel unaccompanied? It is not safe on the streets of the city alone. Where is your mama?"

Darrell's mind still felt fuzzy with sleep. "My mother isn't here. I'm — I'm meeting someone at Leonardo's. I got a little lost yesterday."

The old one narrowed her eyes. "If there were not so much to do, I would take you myself. I do not like to see young women wandering the streets alone. It is not seemly."

"I'll be fine." Darrell tried to make her voice sound convincing. "I have my dog to keep me safe. You told me it isn't far?"

The old woman nodded reluctantly. As she looked like she might be ready to chastise again, Darrell quickly nodded her thanks and hurried off. At the park gate she gave a final wave to the tiny, black figure and followed Delaney through the trees into the grey morning light.

The sun had fully risen by the time Darrell had worked the stiffness from sleeping on a pile of straw out of her arms and legs. In spite of the stiffness, her legs felt rested, and she walked with new energy through the crowds of people going about their morning business. Unaccompanied except by Delaney, she felt many eyes on her, some curious, others strangely hostile. One man, bearing an apparently heavy wooden crate across his back, leered at Darrell and blew a couple of juicy kisses in her direction. She hurried off, beginning to feel quite self-conscious. Just then her attention was drawn to the figure of a large, elegantly dressed man pacing impatiently at the front door of a low, white building.

A stone lion! Darrell stopped for a moment to brush as much of the previous day's dust and straw off her skirts as she could. Delaney at her side, she clutched her walking stick tightly and hurried to stand near the door. Glancing down the lane, she realized the low building was no more than a city block or two from Verrocchio's home. The thought made her groan in frustration.

"A last tour of the city, you say?" The noble's voice thundered, and the servant at the door cowered under his black glance. In spite of the warmth of the early morning, the noble wore a soft scarlet hat and matching cloak trimmed in gold, with a white ruffled collar cascading down the front and a lush fur cape over his shoulders.

"I am the *Duca Lodovico Sforza*, his new *padrone*. He was to meet me here." He raised an imperious eyebrow. "We had an arrangement."

The servant seemed unable to raise his head.

The duke shook a fist in the air. "These artists — they are so temperamental. When he comes to *Milano*, he must put such things aside and create the machines and engines of war he has promised me." He thrust his scarlet cloak to one side and rested one hand on the hilt of his sword.

"He is not here, sire," the servant repeated. "All his belongings have been sent to your lodging in the *Piazza Del Duomo*. He said his farewells yesterday. I expected he would stay last night with you, Your Excellency."

All his things packed? Any plan she'd had of getting a look at Leonardo's notebooks evaporated, and Darrell slumped against the wall. Delaney pushed his head into her hand, but she could find no comfort in the touch of his soft fur. *Milan!* She racked her brain. *Why had Leonardo gone to Milan?*

"Ah. All is well, then. He must be waiting for me at my lodgings." The noble spun on his heel to leave, side-stepping abruptly to avoid bumping into Darrell. He muttered something low in his throat, and was gone with a swirl of his cloak and a clank of his sword. His carriage rattled off down the lane.

There was only one hope left. If she could speak with Leonardo before he left, perhaps she could somehow persuade him to tell her his theory of time travel. She stepped forward and put her hand on the door before the servant could swing it closed.

"Excuse me, *signore*. I have a message for Leonardo from — from his old teacher Verrocchio. I must get it to him before he leaves."

"I'm sorry, *signorina*. As I told the duke, Master Leonardo has already left. He said he wanted to spend time taking a final glimpse of the city that has been his home for so many years."

Darrell nodded. "Yes, I heard. But if you can tell me where the duke is lodging, perhaps I may find your master there."

"The duke has rooms in the *Piazza Del Duomo*. It is not far, just down the lane to the *piazza*. Look for the cathedral dome."

Darrell's heart lifted. She repeated the directions to the duke's lodgings and set off into the growing warmth of the morning, Delaney wagging his still muddy tail.

Darrell located the *piazza* easily enough, for the dome could be seen for miles in every direction. It was clearly the tallest structure in this part of Florence, and she had passed it several times yesterday. Her fingers itched for her charcoal and paper as the morning cast its light on the vivid colours of the beautiful city. But all thoughts of drawing evaporated as she stepped onto the cobble-stoned surface of the square in front of the dome and saw the duke's carriage pulled up in front of an elabo-rately designed house along one side of the square. As she began to cross the busy *piazza*, Delaney barked and tore off in the other direction.

Darrell hurried after the dog as he headed around the corner, thinking that she was going to need to find a leash if he kept running off like this. In the long shad-ow cast by the dome of the cathedral, she could see

Delaney seated at the feet of a striking man of about thirty, balding on top but with long, reddish-brown hair caught up in a ponytail at his neck. The man sat on a stone bench outside the cathedral, breadcrumbs scattered at his feet. A tall nobleman with tousled dark hair and mud-spattered clothes stood next to him.

Her heart thumping, Darrell walked slowly to the bench.

"Your dog has frightened away all my pigeons," the seated man said, running his hand along Delaney's back fondly, nonetheless.

Darrell felt tongue-tied. She could see only a glimpse of the boy from her first journey in the man he had become. After searching for so long, now that she had found him it was as if her words had deserted her.

"Sir, I have been looking for you for two days," she said, trying to keep the desperation out of her voice.

"Have you?" He lifted his large hand off the dog's head and gestured at the sky. "I have been walking through my city," he said, swinging his hand down and patting the bench, "and saying goodbye to an old friend."

Leonardo looked more closely at Darrell as she sat down gratefully. "Are you the daughter of Don Genova? Or perhaps Don Corleone? I feel that I know your face." He looked around. "And where is your chaperone? Surely you do not travel alone in this vast city?"

Darrell swallowed uncomfortably. "My parents are in — in the Duomo, praying for our safe return to Verona," she said, feeling her face flush. "I crept away when I saw you seated here, hoping that I might steal a moment of your time."

Leonardo's face was melancholy. He gazed unsee-ingly for a moment into the busy square, but when he spoke his voice was harsh. "Why is it you seek me out and do not allow a man to bid farewell to his home and his friend in peace?"

"I just wanted to ask about your work," she said, feeling unsure how to begin. "But — can you tell me first why you are leaving Florence?"

"It is time to move on. My work is no longer *apprezzato* — appreciated in this place." He snapped his fingers dismissively.

Darrell felt surprised. "How can you say that? Look at all you have accomplished…"

"It is as nothing," he interrupted. "My *padroni*, the Medici family, turn their attentions to the upstart Michelangelo. He is not even from *Firenze*. They show-er his works with attention and money. Pah!" He spat on the ground.

Darrell carefully tucked her long skirts out of the way and decided this was not the time to remind Leonardo that he had been born in the nearby town of *Vinci* and was no more a native of *Firenze* than she.

From off his shoulder he drew a finely wrought leather satchel and rummaged around inside to produce a plain leather notebook, with an ornate letter "L" raised in relief on the cover. He tossed the satchel in her lap and flourished the notebook. Two pens, some red chalk, and a small bottle of ink dropped out of the bag, and she clutched the satchel to stop it from falling. The ink bottle shattered, spraying Leonardo's boots. He kicked the shards of glass away impatiently.

"This morning these notes were returned to me, after being stolen to be sold to the highest bidder. Perhaps it was the upstart Michelangelo who tried to steal my ideas. Who knows? My thoughts, my dreams — nearly stolen forever. But thanks to my oldest friend, Giovanni, they are back safe in my keeping."

Of course! Darrell looked again at the tall noble, and the memory of his teenage features and vivid blue eyes came flooding back. *His eyes remind me of his grandfather,* she thought, a strange feeling settling into her stomach.

Leonardo brandished the notebook under Darrell's nose. "See all that was nearly lost to me?" He flipped through the pages like a man possessed. "A complete underground waterworks system — a furnace fired by hydraulics — a cross-bow that can kill many men with a single shot — a flying machine."

"My friend, you must take better care with your ideas — and your notebooks." Giovanni spoke to Leonardo but grinned at Darrell. "Just last evening, I had to take back this very notebook from an unscrupulous criminal. He was ready to sell it to some cheap imitator of my friend's ideas, and it was no easy task to dissuade him." He clasped Leonardo by the hand. "Guard your secrets well, my friend. There are many who would pay a fine coin to see your deepest musings and your private projects."

Giovanni caught Darrell's gaze once more with his vivid blue eyes and smiled. "Did you miss your most amiable companion last evening?" he asked, as he reached over and ruffled Delaney's fur. "For when I most had need of help, I turned and found him by my side."

"*My* dog?" Darrell reached over to stroke Delaney's soft head and remembered her long wait for him by the fire at the wedding.

Giovanni stood and struck a self-mockingly dramatic pose, though he had trouble suppressing a grin. "When my friend told me of the stolen notebook and of the threat to sell it, I was incensed. I leapt on my horse and galloped off to stop this nefarious deed."

Leonardo rolled his eyes at Darrell. "I was packaging up my belongings, so I begged him to go in my stead."

Giovanni raised his eyebrow. "Do not ruin a good story, Leo." He cleared his throat dramatically and gazed off into the distance. A small girl, her clothes black with dirt, crept away from the skirts of her mother, who was begging on the steps of the cathedral. The tiny girl stood with her mouth open and her eyes glued to Giovanni.

"On I rode through the darkness, fear in my heart, until at last I came upon the small inn where the villain had said he would meet Leonardo. As I tied my horse outside, your friend here," he looked down fondly at Delaney, "crept up beside me and put his head under my hand. It was as if he had arrived to help me in my quest." Several other children gathered around Giovanni's feet, and his eyes twinkled briefly at Darrell before he resumed his narrative.

"The inn was dark, and stank of sour ale, spoiled food — and worse. A small fire that crackled in a soot-smudged fireplace provided the only light. Uncounted numbers sat around in the dark, drinking ale and muttering. I called for the innkeeper to bring out his lamp, but just as he set the thing on the long wooden counter, the door blew open and a wind, cold as death, whistled through the room."

The tiny girl at Giovanni's feet gasped. Leonardo shook his head indulgently. "Get on with it, if you must," he said gruffly, trying unsuccessfully to disguise his own interest.

Giovanni bent over, clearly playing to his rapt audience. "'It's not a time for light, but for darkness,' came a voice from the doorway, and silence dropped over the room like a shroud."

He puffed up his chest and resumed his heroic stance. "'I do not fear to show my face in the light,' I said, and looked around the assembled company."

Giovanni turned his glance to Darrell, clear blue eyes aglow. "I readied myself for the bargaining when who should pad in through the open doorway but my friend here. He leaned firmly against my knee. As we stood bathed in the light of the fire, shadows dancing wildly on the wall behind us, I knew all would be well, for I had a noble partner in this terrible endeavour."

The crowd gathered around Giovanni's feet nodded and smiled at each other appreciatively.

He pulled his features into a vicious grimace. "The voice from the door snarled 'Get that stinking cur out of here.' Something caught the corner of my eye, and I turned my head in time to see a clay pint pot flying through the air at the dog. I caught the pint pot with ease, and swung it onto the worn wooden table that served as a counter."

Giovanni bent down and lifted one of Delaney's ears. The dog's tail thumped. "'In the corner, *mia cane*,' I whispered, and stood up to face the man at the door. I recognized him. His name is Salvatore and he is known in *Firenze* as a petty thief and a pickpocket. A young man but not a good man. I knew when I looked in his eyes that I would need all the wiles of my own brain and that of my noble partner to triumph.

"'You bring a cold wind, Salvatore. Is it bad news you have for me as well?' Salvatore sneered and stepped into the lamplight. I could see his dirt-streaked face, marked with a livid red scar searing across one cheek and down his jawline. He is no older than I, but clearly his years have been hard.

"'I hope it's gold you have brought for me tonight, *mio signore*,' he spat, 'or the news will be nothing but bad.' He ducked his head toward the dark corner. 'That dog marks you, *signore*. And one thievin' beast exposes another, so they say.'

"I laughed at him. 'The dog belongs to a friend, and he's simply here — to keep me company.' I pointed at Sal's smirking face. 'From the look of you, you've fought a recent battle or two since I've seen you last.'

"Salvatore's mouth pushed more deeply down at the corners, if that be possible, and he spat a wad of phlegm into the straw at the my feet. 'Just nicked m'self as I sent a lesser man to his maker,' he whispered. 'He arrived without the gold he promised me, and paid the price for his mistake.'"

Giovanni wrinkled his nose. "The fellow sickened me with his smell, and I had no further patience for his words. 'I have your gold, man. Have you got that which I seek?'

"'Maybe so. The gold first, *mio signore.*' He stuck his hand in my face."

Giovanni straightened his back and narrowed his eyes. "'I don't pay for what I can't see.' Salvatore snarled and spat again, but he pulled a slim volume out of his sleeve. My heart leapt! I took the book, gently opened it, and traced my finger over the name inscribed on the flyleaf."

Leonardo grinned up at Giovanni. "Success at last, my good friend!"

Giovanni shook his head. "Not yet, I fear. I flipped through the book and the firelight danced on the pages. I turned to Salvatore.

"'This is a prize worth more to me than jewels,' I told him, and tossed the small bag of coins you had given me, Leonardo. The bag clinked as it landed at his feet and he dropped to his knees to retrieve it.

"The bag disappeared into the same sleeve from which the book had come. For the first time he broke into a grin himself, his mouth missing more than half its teeth, the others black with rot."

The children groaned appreciatively, but Giovanni shook his head.

"Alas! My joy at finding the book led me to forget to remain alert. While I read through Leonardo's notebook, Salvatore spoke. 'Did I not mention the price has increased?' he chortled, and I became all too aware that two of his cronies had crept up behind me, as I felt the sharp point of a knife behind each ear."

The children gasped in horror, but Leonardo leaned back on the bench and raised his eyebrows.

Giovanni's face took on crafty expression, and as he gazed down over his audience, he flexed his knees slightly. "I showed nothing on my face, but readied myself for whatever was to come. I looked down at Sal, chuckling and still on his knees in the filthy straw that covered the dirt floor.

"'I know you to be a man without honour,' I said quietly. 'I should have expected no less.'

"'You should have known better,' he mocked me, struggling to his feet. 'But a greater man than you has need of this same prize.' He snatched the volume out of my hands. 'Yet, why either of you value words over gold, I cannot fathom.' He jerked his head, and the two men with knives clutched my arms with iron grip. 'You know what needs be done,' he told them. 'The usual spot.'"

Giovanni grinned and held his arms back to show how he had been pinned. "My arms felt close to breaking, but I gave no sign. 'The usual spot, Sal? Don't you have a more special place planned — for me and my dog?'"

He gave a piercing whistle and the whole group jumped. Delaney sat up alertly and the children laughed. "From the dark corner a missile came flying, planting two front paws between Sal's shoulder blades. Salvatore went down hard, his head glancing off the flagstone hearth. Taking advantage of my moment of surprise, I gave a mighty heave of my arms," Giovanni mimed this action to the delight of his audience, "and with a sickening crack, smashed together the skulls of the two men who held me. They slapped to the floor like dead codfish."

The children laughed aloud and one little boy clapped his hands enthusiastically.

Giovanni grinned. "I shook out my tingling arms and scooped the book out of the straw. Stepping over the prone bodies of the men on the floor, I strode to the door of the inn, the dog at my heels. I looked back at the scene behind me: two thugs unconscious on the floor, and Salvatore struggling to his feet with filth and straw all over his clothes.

"'Keep the gold, Sal. I always pay my due.'

"Salvatore looked down at the two bodies still prostrate on the grimy floor. 'Some filthy book, all marked over in unreadable scrawl.' He shrugged. 'But still — I believe I got the best of the bargain.'"

Giovanni grinned at the group, now numbering at least twenty. "As my friend here will confirm, I could not agree less."

He looked down at Darrell. "Outside I mounted my horse and called to the dog. '*Mia cane*! Time now to ride like the wind and return this prize to my friend, so that he may continue his work in peace.' And you know," he added, his voice low, "the dog barked just as if he understood my words and chased my galloping horse all the way home through the black and windy night."

He bowed flamboyantly and sat down on the bench beside Darrell to much cheering and applause.

As the crowd dispersed, Leonardo rolled his eyes at Darrell again. "This is what I get for having an actor for a friend," he complained good-naturedly.

Giovanni ruffled Delaney's fur. "I do thank you again, *signorina*. He reminds me of a dog who once used to visit my grandfather. Keep by his side. He is a most — helpful beast."

He stood abruptly and clapped Leonardo on the shoulder. "I am away, *mio amico*, to see to my own business. I wish you well on your journey, and I will come and help you set up your studio in Milan next month, mmm?"

Leonardo nodded and waved as his friend strode off. Delaney jumped to his feet and barked once before returning to his spot beside Darrell.

Darrell swallowed. She had learned much about Leonardo's life from books, but seeing him here, sitting beside her — he was more real than the man she had read about. His notebook proved he was a sculptor, a painter, a mechanic, a physicist, a designer, an architect, and so much more. But what of his "secret project" — the time machine? The notebook was not complete, and Darrell could see several blank pages near the end. "It looks like you still have room for more ideas," she ventured. "Why do you need to move away?"

"I can't seem to get anything finished here," he complained. "My mind is so full, there are not hours in the day enough to make the smallest dent in the ideas racing through my brain." He leapt to his feet and Darrell followed, still clutching the satchel, frantic with worry that he would brush her aside and return to the lodging of the duke.

"I am in constant fear of the competition here. Lesser artists — they will stop at nothing to have a taste of what my mind can provide." He walked back along the street, the way Darrell had come, rather than toward the duke's lodgings. A sliver of hope glimmering in her chest, she hastened behind, and soon they were walking down the tree-lined lane leading to his studio and, further along, to Verrocchio's home.

"In *Milano*, I will be better able to accomplish great things. My new patron, Duke Sforza, will have all the war machines he can possibly use, and I will have time to spend on my most exciting project ever."

Darrell's heart pounded. *The secret project!*

He brandished his notebook and grinned. "When this new project comes to light," he said, his expression suddenly boyish, "people everywhere will say 'Leonardo' when the word they mean is 'genius'."

In spite of her excitement, Darrell rolled her eyes. Leonardo the man seemed so different from the boy, but his ego certainly hadn't diminished over the years. "Don't they believe that already?" she asked, her voice dry.

Leonardo carried on as though she hadn't spoken. "They will see me in the streets of *Milano* and they will say, 'Now there goes a man who has changed the world.'"

The low stone building soon appeared, and Darrell followed Leonardo around the back, trying to keep her footing on the rough cobblestones and still keep up with his long stride. She was concentrating so hard she only narrowly missed crashing into him when he stopped suddenly in front of her.

"Look at this," he whispered, and pointed to a muddy ball of twigs and branches tucked into the corner of a tree. The gnarled tree grew near a window of the back wall of the studio.

Leonardo's voice dropped to a gentle croon. He leaned against the wall and slowly stretched out his hand. Darrell held her breath. A tiny bird hopped into

Leonardo's open palm, and he drew his hand close for Darrell to see. The bird shivered but held perfectly still, eyes of brilliant black darting.

"I have spent many months cultivating a friendship with this *uccello*," Leonardo breathed, his strident voice of a moment before now dropped to the timbre of a whispered breeze. "This small creature has much more to teach me than I could learn in a dozen lifetimes. I have watched her build her nest on this windowsill, carrying mouthfuls of mud for weeks and spitting them into place, cementing the twigs and leaves she has carried in her beak. The architecture!" He smiled. "The design of the place. So compact, so perfect for the upbringing of her *uccellini*."

He passed his notebook to Darrell with a nod. "You can see in these pages I made many sketches to document her progress in building this work of art she lives in with her small family." He smiled again at the bird. "And the process of learning to fly! Just as I felt I may be able to do justice to her hard work in a painting, she pushed her *uccellini* from the nest." He rested one finger on a twig and the tiny bird hopped off his hand and ran up the branch to her nest.

Darrell turned the pages of the notebook with trembling fingers. It was jammed with words and half-finished drawings, studies of animals and birds. Near the back, a series of designs of some complicated machinery filled several pages. And on one page, three words were written repeatedly in both regular and mirror script, and trapped in a spiderweb of connected lines: *Tempo, Spazio, Luce.*

Time. Space. Light.

Darrell suddenly felt wobbly all over. Could this be the answer? Clutching the book tightly, she shook her head to clear it and realized that Leonardo was still speaking about the tiny birds.

He continued as though in a dream, his voice soft. "I was mesmerized. How did she know they were ready? How did they learn? What kept them aloft? I had to know!"

He strode to the studio door and flung it wide.

Darrell followed him inside. *His mind jumps from one topic to the next like quicksilver. No wonder he never gets anything done.* She stepped forward into a large room, the like of which she had never seen before.

It was a total mess. Large lumps of clay sat in one corner, a damp cloth thrown carelessly over top. Another corner held great mounds of broken crockery. The floor was strewn with dust and blotched with vast smears of paint. At least four easels displayed canvasses in various stages of completion, and a strange Rube Goldberg-like contraption made out of soldered iron stood in the centre of the room.

Leonardo strode over to a heavy oak table, the top of which was stacked high with paper and parchment, canvas and cloth. With one large hand, he swept the surface clean and with the other he grabbed the satchel from Darrell. Reaching inside, he pulled out a rolled page and spread it wide on the now-cleared surface.

His face softened. "One *piccolo uccellino* misjudged the branch one day and fell. I ran out to find his wee body on the ground beneath the window, still shaking, still quivering."

Darrell was astounded to see Leonardo's eyes redden.

"I picked up the wee babe and it died in my hand. It had failed to learn the lesson nature and its mother had tried to teach. I was determined the death of the bird would not be in vain. I carried the small corpse to this very table and began a complete anatomical study." He pointed to the page he had pulled from the satchel, depicting several detailed sketches of the anatomy of a small bird.

"You cut it up?" For a moment Darrell forgot about the notebook she held as her heart filled with outrage. "You took the poor dead hatchling and you cut it up?"

Leonardo, his own tenderness of the moment before apparently forgotten, looked annoyed.

"Of course I cut it up, ridiculous girl. I needed to see the way the feathers were attached and how the bones were formed if I wanted to learn how it could fly."

"But it couldn't fly! That's why it died!" Darrell couldn't believe what she was hearing. "Don't you care that it was once a living creature? You only studied it so you could figure out how to build an airplane." She clutched the book to her side and glared at him.

Leonardo glared right back at her, his thinning hair bristling around his head in a red halo. He opened his mouth, apparently ready to bellow back at Darrell, and then closed it abruptly with a snap. "Air — plane?" he muttered quietly.

Darrell bit her lip. *Oh-oh.*

"Air — plane. A plane — a smooth, angled plane flying through the air." He looked up, a quizzical expression on his handsome face. "I think you may have given me an idea, *bambina*," he said softly. Without another word, he dropped into a chair by the table. Pulling over a piece of parchment, he dipped his pen into an open inkwell and began to write from right to left at an astonishing rate.

He lifted his head briefly and met Darrell's eyes with his own. "Leave me. I must finish these notes right away before I ready myself for the journey." He flapped his arm at Darrell as though she were an annoying insect.

"But sir — the duke?"

Leonardo shook his head impatiently. "The duke may have my soul tomorrow," he said, dipping his pen and giving Darrell a ferocious grin, "but today, my thoughts and my time are my own. Be gone!"

His head dropped back to his work, and Darrell crept out of the room.

CHAPTER TEN

It was not until she reached the back garden that Darrell realized she still clutched Leonardo's notebook.

"Look at this, Delaney," she said, dropping to sit on a garden bench. Opening the book, she was thrilled to see that while most of it was taken up with sketches, short passages of his recognizable handwriting were scattered throughout. Flipping the pages, she realized that she could read the Italian words, but only painstakingly, as the whole thing was in mirror script. It was going to take a long time to copy down all these notes. It was almost noon, and she was tired and sore and ready to go home.

Forget writing this out. She felt warm in the reflected sun and that made her sleepy again. "He'll never miss it — he has dozens. I'm going to take it with me," she whispered to the dog as they got to their feet. "Come on, Delaney. Let's go home."

The route back to Verrocchio's house was easily retraced, and Darrell limped up to the small stable a short time later. It was lunchtime, and her empty stomach rumbled. The doors to the house were closed, though the window shutters had been thrown open to let in the warmth of the fall day. She lifted the beam barring the stable door, every bone and muscle in her body aching with weariness. Delaney led the way into the darkened stable, and Darrell could hear the pony shift in his stall and blow softly.

Leaving the door ajar for the light, she followed Delaney inside. Darrell tucked the notebook into her pocket and closed her fingers around the few mints remaining from her journey of the day before. She realized the ache she felt in her stomach might have something to do with the fact she hadn't eaten anything since her meal at the wedding party, which now seemed like an eternity ago. She popped in a mint and then, stepping carefully, held out her hand to let the pony nuzzle another. "Thanks for letting me use your stable," she said, as he crunched up the candy and blew gently in her hand for more.

Delaney trotted up the steps, neatly hopping the broken riser and spun in a circle at the edge of the tiny loft. "You sure don't look very tired," Darrell whispered as she started up the stairs, holding the edge of the beam above for balance. She paused and gazed thoughtfully at the broken stair before stepping over it, her eyes on Delaney. As she swung her foot onto the floor of the loft, Delaney pushed his head under her hand and they were swept into the torrent.

The thin sun of an early winter afternoon beamed in through the glass of the lantern room as Darrell awoke. Her head hurt a little, but the mint she had tucked in her cheek before the whirlwind drew her in worked its usual magic on her nausea. There was no sign of Delaney, and she sat up suddenly, remembering the prize in her pocket. She grabbed the windowsill and hauled herself up slowly, every muscle sore. But what about the small notebook? After a moment's search she found it, nestled in the back pocket of her jeans.

Darrell pulled it out of her pocket and turned it over gingerly. It looked so old! The cover was cracked and brittle, and the pages inside seemed as thin as onion skin. Still, each page was covered with words and pictures in spidery ink gone sepia with age. She felt a twinge of guilt at stealing the book that Giovanni had gone to such great pains to rescue. Still — she pushed the guilt resolutely aside. Fragile or not, she knew this notebook contained Leonardo's secret project, and perhaps it also held the answers she had sought for so long. Darrell slipped the notebook back into her pocket for safekeeping and hurried to make her way down the stairs.

In the distance, she heard the sound of an engine starting up, and she peeked out the door of the lighthouse with caution. A worker was driving his small Caterpillar towards the lighthouse again, the last roll of fencing in the bucket. Behind him a number of other workers straggled down the cliff path, carrying various pieces of smaller equipment.

Darrell decided to make her way around the back of the lighthouse and behind the rocks to the protection of the cliffs. She could hear Delaney whine but didn't want to call him until she was safely away from the lighthouse and out of sight of the workers. She slipped out the door and around the far side of the lighthouse and caught a glimpse of the dog's head.

"What are you doing there, Delaney?" she whispered.

"Good question," said Conrad Kennedy, stepping out from behind the rock.

Conrad let go of Delaney's collar, and the dog came bounding over to Darrell as though shot from a gun. He shivered a little and nuzzled Darrell's hand.

"Did you hurt my dog?" she snarled.

"You call that a dog?" Conrad curled his lip. "Anyway, I didn't hurt him. I just held him by the collar for a minute." He crossed his arms over his chest. "I saw somebody up in the lighthouse, and when I saw the stupid dog running around I knew it had to be you."

Darrell clambered down the rocks. Now she'd been caught, there was no use hiding from the construction workers, and they might prove some protection from Conrad. "Just stay away from me," she said through her teeth. "And leave my dog alone."

"Hey!" The worker driving the Cat jumped out and walked over to Darrell and Conrad. "Were you just in the lighthouse?"

"No —" Darrell began, but Conrad shouted over her voice.

"She was too." He grabbed her roughly by the arm. "I was just watching you guys work and I saw someone walking around upstairs in the lighthouse. I went to check it out and she and her stupid dog were inside."

"There's no need for that," said the worker, and brushed Conrad's hand off Darrell's arm. He turned to Darrell, his tone serious. "If you were inside the lighthouse, then you were trespassing. Where do you live?"

"In Vancouver," Darrell answered. "But I go to Eagle Glen School." She turned her back on Conrad. "I was just taking my dog for a walk," she said to the worker. "I saw all the construction stuff, but I didn't see any 'No Trespassing' signs."

"Ha! What about the 'Private Property' sign on the lighthouse?" Conrad sneered. "Missed that while you were climbing under the chain, I guess?"

"There's no call for that, either." The worker frowned at Conrad. "I think you both need to come with me." They walked along the sand in silence for a few moments until the worker hailed one of the men with equipment.

"Frank! Can you take these kids up to the school? They shouldn't be anywhere near here while all this work is going on." The other worker nodded and walked over.

Darrell looked up and her mouth dropped open. "Uncle Frank!"

"In trouble again, eh?" Frank grinned with the smile that was so much like her own and gave her a hug. He turned to the workman who had brought them from the lighthouse. "I'll take 'em up, Joe. Thanks."

The other worker shrugged and returned to his job.

Frank put out his hand. "Frank Del'Amico. I'm Darrell's uncle, as you might have guessed."

Conrad looked at the hand, scowling. "Yeah, well, your niece is in big trouble. She was hanging around the lighthouse, and that's trespassing."

"Oh yeah?" Frank withdrew his hand and raised his eyebrows at Darrell. He looked back at Conrad. "And what were you doing down there — picking flowers?"

Conrad stuck his hands in his pockets. "I was just out for a walk, minding my own business. I saw somebody messing around in the lighthouse, so I went to check it out. It's not me in trouble, it's her."

"Well, buddy," said Frank, slapping Conrad a little too firmly on the back. "You did a good job. The criminal's been caught and you can head off on your — walk." He grinned and winked at Darrell as Conrad stalked off. "Just make sure you stay off this end of the beach!" he called and turned to his niece. "Nice friends you've got at this school."

Darrell hugged her uncle again. "He's no friend of mine. What are you doing here? Are you working on this job?"

"Yeah, my construction company got the bid to build the new light standard." He slung his arm over her shoulder as they walked toward the path. "I was happy to come down here and have a chance to say hello. So I get here, and what do I find? My favourite niece getting herself into trouble." He grinned and tilted his helmet back on his head. His hair was the same shade of brown as Darrell's, though curlier.

"I'm your *only* niece," she muttered. "But what do you mean construction of the light? I thought they were knocking it down?"

"Oh, they're demolishing the old thing all right," Frank said, puffing a little as he hiked the winding path in his heavy boots. "They're going to replace it with a light on a tower — kind of like a light standard, but a lot higher. Doesn't need as much maintenance. Just gotta change the bulb once in a while." He paused and leaned heavily on a branch of the old arbutus in the garden while he wiped the perspiration off his brow. "They'll take the old one down as soon as the new one is up and running."

"That makes sense, I guess," said Darrell, and yawned hugely.

"Well, honey, I have to get back to work now. You look like you could use a nap, anyway. What's the matter? Your mom drop you off here at the crack of dawn or something?"

Darrell nodded and remembered the secret in her back pocket. "Yeah, we were here pretty early," she agreed. "Maybe I'll go have a little rest."

"Great idea. I'm staying in some little hotel up the highway while I'm on this site, so maybe I can take you out for dinner one night this week."

"Oh — yeah." *I don't have time!* Everything in her rebelled at the thought, but she managed a smile. "I'd — uh — like that a lot."

"Geez, you *must* be tired, kid. Don't think I've ever heard you less enthusiastic about an invitation to eat."

Darrell swallowed another yawn and squeezed her uncle's hand. "G'night, Uncle Frank — I mean, goodbye."

He shook his head and waved. "See you soon, kiddo."

CHAPTER ELEVEN

The next morning, Darrell pulled herself up in her bed and slowly donned her prosthesis, looking carefully at it for what seemed the first time. The top was custom fitted to support her knee and was the latest in lightweight comfort. The foot had a dynamic response and could be adjusted so that she could walk or run with comparative ease. Darrell ran her fingers over the material and thought of the heavy grain of the carved wooden leg she'd worn in Florence.

She reached into the drawer by her bed, pulled out Leonardo's notebook, and slipped it into her backpack. Her leg and the notebook. Something new and something old. And nothing that she understood.

The first bell rang out and she hurried to the door, neatly avoiding conversation with the red-headed spectre that was rising out of Kate's bed.

Darrell turned the slim volume over in her hands. The pages smelled old and strange. After seeing Uncle Frank, she had dropped into her bed and slept until Lily arrived and shook her awake that afternoon. Kate had come in soon after, and the three of them had gone down to meet Brodie and Paris in the dining hall. Darrell had felt muddle-headed and still tired from her long, strange day. She said little, ate her dinner, and returned to her room. The crush of students in the halls between classes had meant she couldn't find a moment of private time, and Kate and Lily's discussion of the upcoming Renaissance fair went on late into the night. She decided to skip the twenty-minute tutorial period after breakfast to sneak up to a quiet carrel in the library.

Darrell had slipped the notebook into a plastic bag for protection, and now, at her desk in the library, she unwrapped it carefully. She set it gently on the table beside a larger book pulled from the library shelves. Inside the front cover, the first page was blank, except for a name written backwards:

The pages beneath her fingers reminded Darrell a little of her own notebooks: filled with jottings, scrawls, and a multitude of sketches in various stages of completion. The strange mirror writing ran throughout the book. When Darrell slipped her pocket mirror out of her pack, her fears were confirmed. At Eagle Glen, at least, her ability to read Italian script was limited to Leonardo's name on the front page. *This won't be a problem. There are tons of translation services on the Internet. I may not get all of it, but I'll be able to find out the general ideas.*

With shaking fingers she flipped the pages and looked at the final sketch. It was a complicated machine with many gears, levers, and what appeared to be a sort of helicopter wing on the top.

"This has to be it," she muttered aloud. "Now I just need to find out how it works."

She dragged her attention to the larger library book and pored through the index, determined to find what she was looking for. Absorbed in the words from the library book, she clutched Leonardo's notebook tightly in her lap and hardly noticed her hands were trembling.

Night fell earlier as the term wore on, and it was particularly black outside the study room windows as Darrell sat at a table, absorbed in her research. She had ignored Kate's puzzled frown when Darrell had declined to sit together and pulled her chair into a quiet corner away from the other students. Delaney lay curled on the floor to one side and twitched in his sleep. He was dreaming:

> *waves crashing wind blowing fur*
> *free free free free free*
> *run fast splash paws move run run*

small speck small shape small blur far far far
good girl good girl run
wet wet splash sand toes gritty good gritty

Watching the dog sleep, Darrell saw his eyes darting under their lids and smiled as his feet twitched and pedalled. *Chasing rabbits.* She turned back to her work. But Delaney was not chasing rabbits.

bright hot sand sun run wind run run
scent girl light girl good girl good
dark light grey silver
snuffle leg warm hands gentle girl good
YELP pain pain bite scratch rend hurt hurt
snap bite no no no not girl not girl
snap snarl pain no no bite snap pain
not girl
blood smell pain rocks bite stick bite pain
boy boy hurt pain boy bad pain rocks sticks
sore back teeth sore pain blood stick smell boy
teeth hurt snap whimper...

"Delaney!" Darrell rubbed her hand along the dog's back and his agitated pedalling slowed.

no pain girl girl blood gone
girl there girl pat pat pat no pain
gone bad gone boy gone long gone
girl here good dog girl good dog del aaa nee

"It's only a dream, boy."

He didn't have bad dreams very often, but this one must have been a nightmare, as for a moment he had whimpered and cowered under the touch of her hand. Now he looked up, tail thumping, paw on her foot.

"Hey, keep your dog quiet! We're trying to get some work done over here."

Darrell looked up to see Conrad glaring at her from his table near the door. He was sitting with Paris, and they had a few books open on their table. Darrell could see illustrations of medieval and renaissance instruments.

Paris spoke up. "He's okay, Conrad. It's not bothering anyone."

"Well it's bugging me, so keep him quiet or I'll throw him outside."

Darrell scowled back at Conrad and refused to answer. She reached down and tousled Delaney's furry head before turning back to her work. The dog curled up in a ball once again, this time pushed up tightly against her foot. For another moment, one eye stayed open and he gave a final brief thump with his tail on the floor. Darrell lifted her pen, and his eye slowly closed as he slept soundly once more against the safety of her body.

"Find anything?"

Darrell jumped. "You startled me!"

"Sorry." Kate sat down at the table and reached to pat Delaney as he slept. "So what have you got so far?"

"Uh…" Darrell felt her face go red and she closed her book. "Not much actually."

"Darrell! This is a group project!" Kate's voice dropped to a whisper. "I mean, you're doing Renaissance clothing. How hard can that be? Just write a list of all the clothes you can remember with a short description so the kids in the design class have something to go on when they start sewing the costumes."

Darrell nodded. "Yeah — yeah. I'll work on it as soon as I can."

"I've got a great idea for a game already," said Kate. "I found a site on the Internet that shows how bobbing for apples was common in the Renaissance, so I'm going to set it up as one of the stations." Kate looked at Darrell's notebook, closed on the table. "What *are* you working on, if it's not the clothing?"

"It's nothing. I'm — I'm just finishing my math." Darrell bit her lip to stop from snapping.

"Darrell, we had time in class to finish that. Come and sit over at our table. This is supposed to be a group project, remember?"

"No!" Darrell's temper exploded and suddenly the room was quiet as all heads turned to look at her. "I've got to get this stuff done, okay? I promised you I'd finish the group project stuff later and I will, but *not right now!*"

Kate raised her eyebrows and backed away. "Geez, Darrell, sorry I asked." She walked back to her seat. "She's too busy for us right now," she said sarcastically, but Darrell caught the worried glance passing between Kate and Brodie.

I don't care. She opened her notes again. *I know there's an answer. I'll just have to keep looking.*

Chapter Twelve

Two-thirty in the morning is a terrible time. Especially when it was five hours away from an exam you hadn't begun to study for yet *and* you still had an assignment to finish first. The December sky was black, low clouds obscuring stars and moon. The air in the room felt heavy and cold. Darrell glanced from the darkness outside her window to the clock on her end table and felt something akin to despair.

She had spent weeks working all hours of the day and night trying to decipher Leonardo's notebook. There was no doubt she had made progress. She'd used a site on the Internet to translate all the Italian, and though it was clunky in places, she felt confident she knew what most of the words meant. She'd copied the first words of his notebook into her own: *He turns not back who is bound to a star.* But the rest of the ideas described were so scattered, she could hardly make any sense out of them at all. And the diagrams! Leonardo's sketches were beautiful and carefully rendered, but they didn't correlate with his written work in any way she could understand. And there was nothing about a time machine anywhere.

"He must have been writing in code," she muttered.

Kate stirred in her bed. "Turn off the light," she complained, her voice almost completely muffled by her pillow.

"Okay, okay, go back to sleep," muttered Darrell, and reached to turn off the light. She could always put it on again in a few minutes when Kate went back to sleep.

"What are you up to, Darrell?" Kate's voice, thick with sleep, came through the darkened room.

"Nothing. Studying. Go back to sleep."

"At two-thirty in the morning? Are you crazy?"

"Okay, okay, I'll lie down for a few minutes if it'll get you to leave me alone."

Kate sat up in bed, a dark shadow in the corner. "This has gone on long enough." All the sleep dropped from her voice and she wrapped her shoulders in her blanket and padded across the floor.

"Get off my bed. I'm going to sleep, already. I just need to set my alarm to get up early, so go back to your own bed."

"No." Kate tucked her feet up and wedged herself on the bottom corner of the bed. "I'm not moving until we have a talk, Darrell."

"Oh, come *on*, Kate! Look, you've said yourself we should be asleep. I'll talk to you tomorrow."

"No you won't. You haven't really talked to me for weeks. 'I'm working now' and 'Leave me alone' have become your favourite phrases."

"Well, I've been busy. We've got the test tomorrow and the project and —"

"And, nothing." Kate reached over and snapped on Darrell's tiny book light. "I'm on to you."

"What's that supposed to mean?"

Kate's eyes looked heavy with sleep, but her face was determined. "I know this has something to do with the journey to meet Leonardo, because that's when you stopped having anything to do with us. And I know you've refused to go anywhere near the lighthouse, even just for a walk to look at all the construction down there. You wouldn't even go for dinner with your uncle when he asked!"

"I would have. I just had to finish up some work first. Uncle Frank's not used to waiting for his food."

Kate leaned forward and stared into Darrell's tired eyes. "Something is going on, I know it. So spill the beans or else."

"Or else what?"

"Or else — I'm going to tell Professor Tooth everything. Darrell, you are acting exactly like you did after the accident when you turned your back on everyone at home in Vancouver. I know what you're really like, and it's not this. I think she might be able to help."

Darrell slumped back in her bed against her pillow. She was so tired she felt she didn't have a single argument left inside her. "Professor Tooth probably knows everything already," she said numbly. "And nothing is going the way it was supposed to, so I guess it doesn't matter anyway." She looked into a dark corner so Kate wouldn't see the tears of frustration and exhaustion welling in her eyes.

"Look, Darrell, I'm really tired too. I can give you a little good news, though. You don't have to worry about the group project."

"What do you mean?"

"I mean Brodie did your section for you. He's worried about you, too, y'know." Kate reached over and put her hand on Darrell's arm. "You are our friend. If something's bugging you, you're supposed to tell us, so we can at least try to help."

Darrell sniffed but couldn't speak.

"Is it Conrad? I know he's been hanging around a lot lately, but maybe it's his way of trying to fit in. Paris tells me Connie's doing really well in music lately, and he hasn't been as crabby as usual. I think he might like it here a little."

"It's not Conrad." Darrell sat up and took a deep breath. "Kate — I went back."

Kate nearly slipped off the bed in surprise. "What?"

"It's true." Her words tumbled out. "I went back by myself and I got really lost and I met Leonardo, but he was a grown man and I stole his notebook." Darrell put her face in her hands.

"But — why?"

Darrell dropped her hands. "I read he invented a time machine, and with how we have been able to move through time, I thought he might have really done it. It made sense to me — so I went back to find out the secret."

Kate looked stunned. "But why would you do such a dangerous thing without us?"

Darrell slid her right leg out from under the covers. "Because of this," she said, tears spilling onto her cheeks.

"Because of my leg and my dad." She swiped at her cheek with the back of her hand. "Kate, we can travel through time! We've gone back to medieval times and the Renaissance. There *has* to be some way to control this process. If we can go all the way back hundreds of years, there *has* to be a way for me to go back a few years and stop the accident from happening."

Kate sighed and slumped against the wall at the foot of Darrell's bed. "I had no idea," she said slowly. She dropped the covers from her shoulders, slipped off the bottom of the bed, and walked up to where Darrell was sitting.

"You know, I hardly even remember you have only one foot," she said, bending over to give Darrell a hug. "And I have no concept of how terrible it must be to lose a dad. It makes me sick to think about it." She picked up her blanket again. "We're going to sit down with Brodie tomorrow and talk this thing through," she said with conviction, curling back into her bed. "And if we need to ask Professor Tooth for her help, too, we will. We'll find an answer for you, Darrell, I promise."

Darrell flipped off her light and lay back down in bed. She wiped her face with the edge of her sheet, and her heart a little lighter, tiredness took her and she slept at last.

A fire crackled in the fireplace and a few candles on the old stone mantle bobbed their flaming heads as though to keep time with the beat of the wind on the glass. The test had not been the terrible thing it had grown to in Darrell's mind, and she curled up in the corner of a couch beside the fireplace, the scent of burning cedar in her nostrils and her sketchbook open, ignored on her lap. She had been staring into space but came back to herself as the door to the old study opened with a crash and Brodie came hurrying in.

"Sorry!" he called, in response to the startled looks from everyone in the room. "The wind caught it."

"Mind the candles, dear!" called Mrs. Follett, nervously glancing up from her newspaper at the candles Kate had placed on the mantle.

Brodie pulled up an old wooden chair beside the fire and rubbed his hands together. His fingers looked red and raw, and the cuffs of his jacket were soaked through. The December wind howled around the tower and the rain drove in torrents against the windows. Kate, sitting at a table nearby, shivered and tucked a blanket around her feet. She looked disapprovingly at Brodie.

"You're soaked! What were you doing out on a night like this?"

He grinned and didn't answer directly. The side of his face turned toward Kate remained completely still, but his left eye winked quickly at Darrell.

"I have nothing to say to you, Miss Stick-in-the-Mud," he shot at Kate. He held his frozen fingers to the fire, and Darrell noticed his eyes sparkled with something that could be excitement.

"You've probably been stuck behind a computer screen all day, not even lifting your eyes," he added.

Kate tossed her head. "You couldn't be more wrong. I've been practising my patterns in the gym." She grinned back at him for the first time. "Want me to show you the new flip I've just mastered?"

Brodie shook his head hastily. "I've never had the pleasure of a personal demonstration — and I plan to keep it that way."

Darrell patted the other cushion on her small couch, but Brodie shook his head and pulled his wooden chair closer to the fire. Since the beginning of school, the first-year students had developed somewhat of an evening tradition, a sort of Eagle Glen musical chairs without the music. There were only three old overstuffed chairs in the study room, with the rest of the furniture being of the more utilitarian variety, and most nights the demand for the soft old chairs was high. The room was cozy in spite of its tall ceilings, probably because of the old fireplace, faced with round river rock of many varieties and colours, soot stained and well used. It was kept banked with wood and kindling from an enormous woodpile, which offered occupation to students who unluckily were found at loose ends in the hallways by Mrs. Follett.

"Nothing to do, dear?" she would crow in a triumphant voice, and then haul off the offending loafer for an invigorating hour of wood-chopping and stacking.

"You're up to something," repeated Kate dryly, as Brodie pulled out his notebook and began his homework. "You're soaking wet and you keep changing the subject."

Darrell looked keenly at Brodie, who raised his eyebrows slightly and indicated with a tiny nod of his head the number of other students in the room.

Darrell caught on immediately. "Oh, you know Brodie," she scoffed to Kate. "Always out chasing down one fossil or another. I'm sure he'll show us when he's ready."

Kate finally caught sight of the guarded look in Darrell's eyes and gave an understanding nod of her own. She turned back to the table where her laptop sat blinking and beeping gently and was immediately engrossed in the latest computer program she was developing. As her fingers flew over the keys, she kept up a steady stream of muttering to herself.

Darrell returned to her work. She had almost finished her section of the group project, and late or not, she was determined to pull her own weight and not let her friends down any more than she had already. Today in history class, only she and Conrad had not finished their assignments, but she had spoken to Professor Tooth after the class and promised to have the work completed by the next day. Conrad had curled his lip as he hurtled by her on his way out the door.

A light flared through the windows and lit the room for an instant with a blue flash. Immediately all the lights snapped out. The fire and Kate's candles on the mantlepiece continued to burn merrily, providing only enough light to make out the outlines of the tables and chairs.

"Lightning in December? This is the weirdest weather," Kate complained. Her computer beeped for a moment, then it, too, succumbed to the lack of power. "Rats! Guess I forgot to recharge my battery."

Mrs. Follett was up and bustling around the room. "I'm sorry, but there's not enough light to study by, my dears," she proclaimed, the cheer in her voice clear from a duty night cut irrevocably short. "Let me dig out some emergency flashlights and you can make your way up to your rooms!"

There was a general groan of dismay at this. Power outages were not uncommon on this rugged stretch of coast, and while they usually didn't last long, they often meant an early night for the students.

Mrs. Follett pulled ten or twelve old flashlights from a cupboard near the door. She steered each protesting student into the hall, toward the stairs.

"Now remember to bring those back down in the morning, my dears. You know the rules! No power means early to bed. Good night! Good night!"

In the darkened hallway, Brodie took advantage of the milling students and the bobbing flashlights to hiss in Darrell's ear.

"Library in ten minutes. Bring Kate."

Darrell nodded and squeezed Brodie's arm to show she understood

"Up you go, my dears!" Mrs. Follett insisted cheerily, and then scurried off down the hall toward the office, clutching her flashlight and her tea cup.

Lily appeared beside Darrell and yawned cavernously.

"I'm ready for bed, anyway. I have a practice in the morning to get set for the meet this weekend. We're at the University Pool in Vancouver and their meets are always pretty intense."

Darrell felt relieved. Lily could always be counted on for an early night. It would make tonight's discussion with Kate and Brodie so much easier, and with Lily snoring, their privacy was guaranteed.

With the power off, Lily fell asleep in record time and Kate and Darrell tiptoed out of their room to the sound of her gentle snores less than ten minutes after they had changed into their pyjamas. The wind tore around the old school in noisy gusts and the walls creaked and groaned as the storm hurled its full force against the old building perched on the ragged coast.

Both Darrell and Kate carried flashlights but kept the beams turned off for the trip through the halls. The route was a simple one, as the library stood down the hall and around a corner from the girls' dormitory wing. Brodie's trip, from his room the floor above, would take a few moments longer, so the girls crept through the rows of books and into the "silent study" section near the back of the library to find a place to sit and wait. Delaney followed them like a shadow.

Darrell flicked on her flashlight, illuminating the narrow aisle. "There are no windows back here," she hissed, "so I think we can have a bit of light."

Kate nodded and turned on her own flashlight. Unlike the hardwood floors adorning most of the school rooms, the library floor was carpeted, and in the light of Kate's flash Darrell quickly pulled three chairs together. Kate, wearing the blanket from her bed around her shoulders, hopped quickly into one of the chairs.

"My feet are always freezing," she complained, tucking in her blanket.

Darrell grinned and stuck out her own feet. Her prosthetic foot was unadorned, but she wore a thick sock on her left foot. "If you dressed for the temperature, you'd have less to complain about." She nestled her foot under Delaney's warm fur.

Kate shrugged and craned her neck to look around her chair. "I wonder what's taking Brodie so long?"

"He's got further to come, remember?" Darrell set her flashlight upright on the table. She pulled a notebook out from the pocket of the hooded jacket she wore over her pyjamas and jotted a few words.

Kate leaned over to look. "What're you writing?"

Darrell set down her pen. "I've brought my notes to show you from Leonardo's notebook. And I brought something else, too."

She slid the old notebook, hand bound in dirty leather, across the table. Kate picked it up gingerly. She traced the raised figure on the front with her finger and carefully opened the cover. A few grains of sand spilled out onto the table, and the book opened naturally to a page in the centre, marked with a grimy bit of string.

Kate directed her flashlight at the notebook. "What kind of writing is that?"

Darrell ran her finger along the words, neatly penned on the unruled pages. "It's mirror writing," she whispered. "I watched him do it." She rubbed the pages gently between her fingers.

"It looks handmade," said Kate. "And the paper is strange, kind of oily."

Darrell lifted her eyes from the book. "I think those pages are actually vellum," she said, checking her own notebook. "It was made from very thin calf skin." She reached over and grabbed the flashlight, and held it under her chin as she gently flipped the pages of the book. "They used to make vellum before paper was mass produced."

"Ugh!"

Darrell shrugged and pointed at Kate's watch strap. "What do you think that's made of? Leather is thicker, that's all."

Kate closed the book gently. "It's amazing you were able to bring it back," she said in a low voice.

Darrell nodded. She felt an overwhelming sense of relief to be able to share her thoughts at last. "That's one of the things I want to talk to you about. When I found a fragment of the walking stick Giovanni's grandfather gave me, I got the idea I might be able to bring something back."

"Do you still have it?"

"No, I left it the second time I went back. I couldn't bring it and the book and still hold onto Delaney."

Delaney thumped his tail on the ground and the wind whistled around the school. Kate tilted her head. "Listen to the wind howling. I can't believe Brodie was out in that this afternoon. That guy is crazy."

"Who's crazy?" Brodie popped his head into the circle of light and both girls jumped. Delaney thumped his tail harder and Brodie reached down to scratch his ears.

Kate frowned. "You are — and you scared me! How did you get in here without us hearing you?"

"Practice. I had a little trouble in the upstairs hallway, so I really had to sneak down here quietly."

"Trouble?" Darrell set down her pen. "Did one of the teachers see you?"

Brodie shook his head. "As a matter of fact, it was Conrad."

"What?" Kate craned her neck to look behind Brodie's chair.

Brodie laughed quietly. "It's okay. He didn't actually see me, but when I saw him sneaking around outside my room, I hid behind the portable blackboard they keep in the small alcove at the end of the hall. He poked around a bit, so I stood there until he went back in his room. I waited for five minutes to make sure he was in for good, then I came down."

Darrell felt worried. "What do you think he was doing out there?"

"Who knows?" Brodie shrugged. "But never mind that now. Let me show you something I found today."

Kate smiled triumphantly. "I *knew* you were up to something!"

"Was it in the cave?" Darrell demanded. She still felt like the cave belonged, somehow, only to her, and that anything happening there was her own personal business. "I saw you head over there this afternoon when I was in the art room."

Brodie nodded. "Since my pictures didn't turn out very well, I decided to go back into the cave for another look. I found this." He pulled a small, dirty object out of his pocket and lay it on the table.

Darrell pounced on it. "A stick of chalk! So some-one did draw the lighthouse."

Brodie nodded. "And tonight, before I came up to the study room, I picked up this." He lay a second identical, albeit cleaner, piece of red chalk on the table beside the first.

Darrell stared at the chalk. "From the board in Professor Tooth's office, right?"

"How did you know?"

"I guess I've seen it there, but until you brought this other piece in, it didn't register." She looked at Kate. "Someone wanted us to go to the lighthouse."

Kate nodded. "Professor Tooth?"

Brodie shrugged. "Not necessarily. But it did have to be someone who had access to red chalk like the stuff in the office."

Kate rubbed her eyes wearily. "There is so much about this I don't understand. Who put the lighthouse drawing there? Is it a clue someone left for us to find? How does all this time travel happen, anyway?" She slammed her hand on the table.

"Shhh! Kate, keep quiet," warned Darrell. She put her hand on Kate's arm. "Let's hear Brodie out."

"Listen," Brodie interjected, "all I know is what happened last summer should never have happened according to the laws of physics, chemistry, and any other science I can think of, including logic. But happen it did, we can all vouch for that. And from what Kate told me, you did it again on your own." He looked serious. "Kate gave me the quick version, Darrell, but can you tell me what happened when you went back again?"

Darrell felt shame wash over her. "I'm sorry I've been so awful, Brodie. I was just so sure if I worked hard enough, I could change the past." She slid the ancient notebook across the table and told Brodie the story of her long search for Leonardo's secret.

Brodie listened quietly, nodding, and then surprised Darrell with a question. "Aren't you happy at Eagle Glen?"

"What do you mean? Of course I'm happy here. I love this school."

"Well," he stretched his long legs out from his chair, "if you want so badly to prevent the accident from happening, you may never end up here at Eagle Glen. You will have changed the past — that's got to affect the present."

"Oh. I guess you're right." Darrell sat quiet for a moment, and then put her head in her arms on the table. "It doesn't matter anyway," she said, her voice muffled. "It didn't work."

Brodie nudged her elbow. "Just because it didn't work this time doesn't mean it can't ever work," he said.

Darrell lifted her head. "What do you mean?"

"Well, I'm not sure myself. But if Leonardo did invent a time machine, I think he might be very interested in the true nature of your visit to him." The quiet tone of his voice couldn't cover the enthusiasm. "What if you only went about things the wrong way?"

Kate looked shocked. "You mean she should have told him about where she was really from?"

"Maybe. Or maybe she could do it still." He leaned forward. "Look. We still have a couple of days before the Renaissance fair. What if we get all our work done and then plan to take a trip before the fair? We can take Leonardo's notebook back, tell him the whole story, and find out what he really knew about time travel."

Kate groaned and gestured toward the door of the library, through which the howling wind could still be heard. "Please tell me you don't mean right now!"

"It's all right, Miss Couch Potato, you're safe for the present," Brodie said, chuckling. "We couldn't see anything on a night like this anyway."

"But what about the lighthouse?" Kate's voice was concerned. "The light tower is almost finished. Aren't they supposed to demolish the lighthouse soon?"

Darrell nodded. "Uncle Frank said they would take down the lighthouse as soon as the tower was up and running." She paused. "We'll lose our portal to the past."

"We'll just have to go before that happens," said Brodie. "They don't work on weekends, do they? We'll go on Saturday. That way no one will be around."

"But Saturday is the day of the fair," said Kate. "We can't go then. Everyone will know we're gone."

"We could go Saturday," said Darrell quietly. "All our set-up work is scheduled for Friday, and I'm only on duty Saturday morning."

"I'm off Saturday afternoon as well," said Brodie.

"Well, I'm on Saturday afternoon," said Kate, "but I bet I can switch with Lily."

"Do you think this can really happen?" asked Darrell.

"We'll make it happen," said Brodie firmly. "Or do the best we can to try. Hopefully this storm will blow itself out before our little trip."

Delaney growled low in his throat.

"A little trip to where?" said a harsh voice from the library entrance.

Startled, Darrell shone her flashlight at the figure silhouetted in the doorway.

"I *thought* I saw a light in here. What are you three doing here so late at night? Planning how to get me in more trouble with the principal?"

Darrell slipped the book into her pocket as Brodie spoke. "I don't know what you're talking about, Conrad. We're here giving Kate a little help with some of her — er — homework, and we're done now, anyway. So you can quit worrying about us and go to bed."

Conrad turned his pale gaze onto Darrell. "I know you're up to something," he said, unknowingly echoing Kate's words. "And I plan to find out what it is. I'm sick of being the one who always gets into trouble. I told the professor about your little lighthouse jaunt, Gimpy, and I think she'll be pretty interested to hear how you're spending time when you're supposed to be in bed. Then maybe she'll forget I didn't get my work in today, not that I care about stupid history class, anyway." His eyes gleamed in the light from the flash. "And don't think I didn't see the book you stuffed into your pocket, Gimpy," he sneered over his shoulder. "You should remember to keep track of your valuables. You wouldn't want anything to get lost." He elbowed aside the door and stalked out, leaving it banging on its hinges.

"What did *that* mean?" spluttered Darrell in disgust. "Every time I begin to think he might be turning out okay..." She thought about telling Kate and Brodie about Conrad catching her near the lighthouse, but they'd already started for the door. Besides, she'd already told them how stupid she'd been. Being seen near the lighthouse was just one more mistake.

Kate grinned at Brodie as they stepped out in the hall. "Make sure you lock your room tonight, Brodie. I can't be there to protect you when I'm catching up on my sleep."

"I think I can look after myself." Brodie grinned back and gave Kate a gentle push. "But thanks anyway." He waved goodnight and disappeared into the darkness in the direction of the stairs, as Kate and Darrell walked quietly down the hall to their room.

CHAPTER THIRTEEN

Exams out of the way, final preparations for the Renaissance fair began in earnest. Eagle Glen was awash in noisy activity as stages and equipment were constructed, music practised, and costumes sewed. Professor Myrtle Tooth oversaw all preparations and remained a centre of calm in the middle of the storm. A devastating rain on the Thursday before the fair set things back and alternate venues inside the school were contemplated, but by Friday afternoon, the sun set into a red horizon and forecasts promised clear skies for the rest of the weekend.

Saturday morning dawned to a thin skiff of high cloud floating through a translucent sky. Preparations began early, and in the office Mr. Gill gave Darrell a sheaf of paper.

"Professor Tooth has asked that these information pamphlets be distributed. Since everyone is putting the finishing touches on their areas of responsibility, could you make sure these sheets get handed out?"

"Sure, Mr. Gill."

Darrell hitched up one side of her gown with one hand and carried the handouts in the other. She smiled to herself at the light weight of the emerald green fabric. *This thing is sure a lot easier to move in than the heavy brocade I had to wear in Florence.*

As she emerged out of the front doors, the fair came alive before her eyes. Tents of every conceivable colour and fabric had been erected on the flat area in front of the school. To one side, a jousting pitch had been delineated with flags and streamers. Boris Meirtz, dressed as an English squire, was putting a final coat of silver paint on a pair of wooden swords he had built.

"Nice tights." Darrell handed him his copy of the notice.

Boris blushed bright red. "I tried to come up with something else, but Professor Tooth is giving marks for authenticity, and this is the only thing I could find that squires wore."

Darrell grinned. "That's okay. At least you're not stuck in a long dress."

Boris blinked, and nodded rapidly. Behind him, several students shook sawdust onto the jousting field. Darrell reached over the barrier and handed them each a notice.

"Fair lady?"

Darrell turned to see Brodie standing behind her wearing a big grin and a set of chain mail made from rings pulled off the top of soft drink cans.

"Wow! That must have taken a long time to put together."

He shrugged. "It wasn't so bad. My mom did most of the work. She collected these things in two days at the university and then wired them together. I just had to connect the sleeves to the main body."

Checking over her shoulder for eavesdroppers, Darrell whispered, "Does it feel like the real thing?"

Brodie grinned. "Not really. The closest I came to wearing anything like this was at Ainslie Castle, and their chain mail was a lot rustier *and* a lot heavier, as I recall." He bent his head close to Darrell's. "I'll try to get rid of it for this afternoon. Anyway, I wanted to tell you Kate is looking for you. She's over by the fortune teller's tent."

"Oh yeah! I promised to help Mrs. Follett try out her skills." Darrell stuffed the rest of the notices into Brodie's hands. "Hand one of those out to everyone you see, okay?"

She hurried off as Brodie reluctantly turned on one stirruped heel and began distributing notices to a large group of giggling serving girls setting tables in one of the food tents.

Darrell read the sign on the tent aloud. "*Madame Flora: Seer of all Things Past and Yet to Come.*"

"Great! You made it. Let's go in." Kate wore a grey sweatshirt with a huge rip across the front and an elaborately pleated skirt.

"Elegant outfit."

"I only had time to get half-dressed, okay? I'll get the top on later." Kate danced impatiently from foot to foot. "We'll only go in for a minute. I've still got a few things to get ready, but I promised we'd help out."

Darrell rolled her eyes. "It's only Mrs. Follett, dressed up as a gypsy. We may find out when the next school newsletter will be sent home, but that's about all."

Kate sighed with exasperation. "Look, I've only got twenty minutes before I have to go back on duty at my booth. It's just to give Madame Flora some practice."

Darrell shrugged and slid inside the tent, Kate following close behind.

"You go first. I'll stand back here," Kate said, and pushed Darrell toward the woman seated at a small table inside the gloomy tent.

Darrell sat down in an old wicker chair. The table was covered with a black cloth, garishly embroidered with the signs of the zodiac, moons, and stars in gold thread. A glass globe sat atop a ragged rip in the cloth, imperfectly concealing a flashlight secreted underneath. The dark interior of the tent smelled of mothballs, making Darrell's eyes water.

Madame Flora adjusted her turban, which waggled dangerously as the girls made their way into the tent. "Cross my palm with silver," she began in a quavery voice.

Darrell rolled her eyes at Kate but managed to fish around in the leather purse she had tied at her waist to come up with a dollar.

"I think I've only got a loonie," she said, apologetically, "and I know it's not made of silver."

Madame Flora smiled. "I'm sure it will be fine, dear," she said, tucking the coin into the pocket of her royal purple bathrobe.

"Wait — wait — I've got silver," said Kate, and hurriedly stuffed an old quarter in Darrell's hand. Darrell passed the quarter to Madame Flora, who dropped it quickly into her jangling pocket.

"Thank you, dear," Mrs. Follett whispered into the corner.

"Happy to help," Kate whispered back.

Mrs. Follett resumed her role as Madame Flora and gazed meaningfully at Darrell. "Let me look into the glass and see what visions I can call forth from the future," she intoned, her voice a full octave deeper than normal. She struggled briefly under the table until, with a click, a dim light shone from the crystal ball.

"Your future appears very bright, dear," Mrs. Follett began, once again forgetting her gypsy persona. The flashlight flickered once and went out.

Darrell snorted. "So much for my bright future."

"Wait a moment — wait — one — moment," insisted Mrs. Follett, still fiddling under the tablecloth. The light would not go back on.

"I'm afraid my battery has died, dear," she said sadly.

"Oh, Madame Flora," Kate implored. "Can't you read tarot cards or some tea leaves or something?"

Darrell grinned. "That's all right, Madame Flora. It's time we got back to our jobs, anyway."

"Well, dear, you *did* give me the donation. Let me read your palm, in exchange." She looked conspiratorially at Kate. "I've just read a new book from the school library on the subject, and I'd love to give it a try."

A vision of piercing blue eyes floated through Darrell's brain. She swallowed. "I — I'm not sure…"

Kate poked her in the back. "C'mon, Darrell. It's just for fun."

Darrell glared at Kate, but lay her hand, palm up, on the table.

"Now let me see," began Madame Flora, squinting though the dim light inside the tent at Darrell's palm.

"Will this help?" Kate said, and hoisted the tent flap to let in a wash of cool air and thin December sunshine.

"Thank you, dear." Madame Flora put on her reading glasses and peered at Darrell's open hand. "Hmmmm. Well. This is certainly very strange. Well, well, well." She looked at Darrell over the top of her reading glasses.

"Is it something really cool?" whispered Kate. "Will she marry a tall, handsome stranger with blue hair?" She broke off, dissolving in laughter.

"No, I don't see that," said Madame Flora, and her face creased with worry. "It's your lifeline, dear. I don't recall seeing one quite like it in the book."

"What do you mean?" asked Darrell.

"It's so — so branched. The book said broken life-lines are quite common and do not necessarily indicate a short life. But this — well, perhaps it means you will have many careers in the future. That must be it." Madame Flora nodded firmly.

Darrell began to pull her hand away and rise, but Madame Flora, with a twinkle directed at Kate, pulled her back down into the seat. "We have to check your love life, dear. That is an essential part of having your fortune told."

"Yeah, Darrell," Kate chimed in. "Let's see if we can find that good-looking stranger in your future."

Mrs. Follett smiled, and without even looking at Darrell's hand she gave a little cough and resumed the deep voice of Madame Flora. "You will find great love in your life, and — and — great…" she paused and looked down at Darrell's palm for further inspiration.

"Money?" interjected Kate, hopefully.

"No — no, dear, that's not it." Madame Flora gazed into Darrell's palm for a moment and then, looking very flustered, pulled off her turban, instantly becoming Mrs. Follett again. She squeezed Darrell's hand and got to her feet. "I'm afraid I'm not very good at reading the future," she said, patting her flattened hair with nervous fingers. "I think I should go help out with the apple bobbing."

Darrell gave a forced smile. "That's okay, Mrs. Follett. I know it's all in fun, anyway." She watched the school secretary struggling to get out of her bathrobe. "Let me help you with your sleeve."

"Oh, thank you, dear. Yes, the apple bobbing booth is really the place for me. Much less upsetting. Come to think of it, with all the water over there I should probably be keeping this bathrobe on."

Darrell glanced at Mrs. Follett thoughtfully. "Yes, maybe you're right about that. Um, Mrs. Follett, what did you mean by the apple bobbing being *less upsetting*?"

Kate, who was still holding the tent flap open, let it fall, and the rank, dim light of the tent swallowed them once more.

"Oh, it's all nonsense, anyway," said Mrs. Follett, but she paused with her hand on the chair.

Darrell gave a short, forced laugh. "I know what you mean," she agreed, "but what was the last thing you saw in my palm? You said *'great love and great ...'"*

Mrs. Follett swallowed. "Well dear — to tell you the truth, I'm not very sure of my own ability in this area. You know," she added with an embarrassed blink, "I only read the palmistry book through the once."

"Oh, I won't take it seriously, Mrs. Follett. I'm just interested — for fun," persisted Darrell.

Mrs. Follett glanced over at Kate and then back at Darrell. "Well if you must know, Darrell, I believe the interpretation would be great love and great — loss."

Kate gave a relieved smile and lifted the tent flap again. "I think Darrell may have gone through that part already," she said, her smile fading as she pointed at Darrell's prosthesis.

"Goes to show you may have been more right than you know," Darrell added lightly.

"Oh, you girls are so understanding," said Mrs. Follett, firmly pinning a "Closed" sign on the outside of the tent. "I promise to give you each a free apple bob to make up for the faulty crystal ball!" She scurried off into the late fall sunlight.

Kate grabbed Darrell's arm. "I thought for a minute she really saw something in your palm," she whispered. Darrell shrugged and shook her head. She was about to respond when Paris came striding up dressed in full minstrel regalia, sky blue from the tip of his curled leather shoes to the short, gold-trimmed cape on his back.

"Wow! Your clothes are brighter than your hair," Kate said, laughing.

Paris slung a mandolin over his back and shrugged. His hair, a natural blonde for once, shone in the morning sun. "Thought you'd be interested to hear who is trying out the stocks, Kate." He grinned. "I know how disappointed you were to hear there were no dunk tanks in the Middle Ages."

"Lily!" Kate shrieked and rabbited off, calling over her shoulder, "C'mon, Darrell, we've only got five minutes for snore revenge!"

Darrell smiled, but lagged a little behind, thinking about the startled look she had seen on Mrs. Follett's face.

The sun was high as Darrell gathered up the last of the sponges to hand over to her replacement. In the end, Darrell's responsibility turned out to be overseeing the stocks, where students who had fared poorly on a Renaissance quiz were required to spend five minutes at the mercy of those students who had scored better as they wielded wet sponges from a distance of thirty paces. The flags on the fairground poles snapped in the wind blowing in from the water.

She peeked at her watch and her stomach clenched. Nearly time to meet Kate and Brodie. She piled the sponges in a bucket.

Paris leaned on the rail and pretended to duck. "I'm on duty, not a victim!"

Darrell forced a laugh and handed him the sponges. "See you later, Paris. Have fun, okay?"

"Okay. Where are you going first? Food?"

"Oh — yeah. I've heard the taffy pull is pretty fun."

Paris curled his lip. "I guess, if you like sticky stuff all over your fingers. I had some kind of meat pie for lunch at the booth over there with the gold and purple flags. It was pretty good."

The last thing Darrell wanted was food. "Okay. That sounds good," she lied. She grabbed her pack from behind the counter. "Where's your mandolin?"

Paris prepared to unlock a student from the stocks. "I gave it to Conrad. He said he'd put it up in my room. Didn't want it to get wet or stepped on."

Darrell couldn't believe it. "Are you crazy?" she began, but Kate staggered up carrying half a barrel. Darrell took one look at her red face and grabbed the other side of the barrel.

"Whew! Thanks. I told Mrs. Follett I'd bring her another one. They're bobbing up a storm over at her booth."

Mrs. Follett waved and walked over, still resplendent, though a trifle damp, in her purple bathrobe. "Wonderful. This will allow me to have two groups bobbing at once." She looked around. "I asked Conrad to help me with the barrel before he left, but he seems to have wandered off."

"He's probably putting away my mandolin," said Paris.

"Stealing it, more likely," muttered Darrell.

Paris laughed. "You need to lighten up on him, Darrell. If you always think the worst of people, that's what you get back from them."

Darrell shrugged and turned to Mrs. Follett. "Did you say 'before he left'? Left where? He should be here helping out." But Mrs. Follett had started back. The girls steadied their load and followed the bustling school secretary. "See you later," Darrell called to Paris.

"Thank you so much, girls," Mrs. Follett twittered, and waved them over. "This is such a help. I could never carry this barrel by myself." She pointed to a spot on the brown grass.

"Where's Conrad gone?" Darrell asked. They set the barrel down with a thud.

"Oh, he's probably gone off to pack, dear," said Mrs. Follett, directing a hose at the apple barrel. "He's been transferred to another school."

Kate grinned. "You're kidding? That's great!"

"How did this happen?" asked Darrell slowly.

"Who cares?" said Kate. "Good riddance. You should be happy to see the last of him."

Darrell made sure she was out of the line of fire from Mrs. Follett's hose. "I don't get it." She paused and looked up at the school secretary. "Are you saying Conrad Kennedy is no longer a registered student in this school?"

"That's right, dear. I got a call this morning from the Youth Corrections Bureau. Apparently they have located his mother in Ontario, and Conrad has been given special permission to return to live with her."

"That's amazing," Kate said, grinning. "No more Conrad."

Mrs. Follett looked disapprovingly at Kate.

"Kate, dear, I expect more of you. Conrad had a few problems, it's true, but that's all in the past. I agree, his father was not a good influence, but he will be under his mother's care now, and I'm sure things will be all right."

She pursed her lips and looked at Darrell. "I hope he will do better with his mother. He's never really managed to settle in here. You haven't seemed to be the best of friends."

"Friends!" Darrell shook her head bitterly. "We don't even qualify as distant acquaintances."

"Well, now he has a chance for a brand new start."

Darrell picked up her bag. "Thanks for letting me know, Mrs. Follett," she muttered, and turned to leave. Struck by an idea, she turned back to the school secretary, now dropping apples into the frigid water in the barrel. "What does Professor Tooth think of this?" she asked quietly.

"Oh, I'm sure she must have approved it," said Mrs. Follett.

"You don't know for sure?" asked Darrell, puzzled.

"Well, I wouldn't have heard from the ministry without Professor Tooth's approval, but I haven't spoken to her about it personally yet, no," said Mrs. Follett. "I've been so busy getting ready for this fair. But the paperwork must be on my desk somewhere."

As the girls walked away, Darrell could hear Mrs. Follett happily directing students to don plastic bibs before they bobbed. Darrell checked her watch. Twelve o'clock. It was time to meet Brodie. She whistled for Delaney and followed Kate behind the school.

CHAPTER FOURTEEN

Darrell gazed along the beach from her perch in the old arbutus tree. "I don't see anybody down there."

"Yeah. I guess the coast is clear." Brodie grinned.

"Ha ha. You're a funny guy," Kate said nervously. "I just want to get this over with and you're making jokes."

Darrell climbed down the tree. "I really want to spend some time talking to Leonardo again. I mean, I want to give him his book back, but…"

"But you want to find out what he knows about time," interrupted Kate.

"And time machines," added Darrell, smiling a little.

"Don't worry, Darrell. This is going to be a piece of cake," said Brodie, walking down the path to the beach. "If we've planned this right, you can get the notebook back to Leonardo and we'll be back practically before we've left."

Darrell watched Kate wiping her hands nervously on her costume. "You guys don't have to come," she said. "I can handle this by myself."

Kate shook her head. "No. You went alone before and you got lost." She took a deep breath. "I can do this. We're your friends, Darrell. We'll go together."

They rounded the last turn and walked out onto the beach.

They hadn't said much on the trip along the deserted beach, and Darrell was lost in her thoughts. What if too much time had passed? Her studies had shown her that after years away, Leonardo had returned to his beloved *Firenze*. But what if Leonardo was no longer in Florence, or worse, if they arrived after his death?

The fence now surrounding the lighthouse seemed designed more to keep debris in than people out, and they easily pushed through a gap in one side. The concrete foundation of the new light standard had been poured and the wooden framing for the rest of the structure was in place.

"I'm going to go up first," said Kate, her voice unsteady. "Less time to change my mind." She ducked under the chain and climbed the stairs two at a time, easily stepping over the broken riser as she made her way up to the lantern room. "The door's closed," she said in a puzzled voice.

"C'mon, Darrell, let's get this over with," said Brodie. He had followed Kate up and stood on the stair below her. "Remember the broken step."

Darrell stopped on the landing and eyed the broken step, speculation swirling her thoughts.

"There's a broken step on the stairs in Verrocchio's stable," she said. "And there was a broken rung on that ladder."

As Brodie reached a hand to help Darrell up the stairs, Delaney squeezed ahead and stood at the top beside Kate. He growled low in his throat.

"Did you close this when you were here?" Kate put her hand on the heavy knob, but the door swung out of her grasp. Light flooded into the twisting stairwell from the lantern room above.

"Now, this is interesting," said Conrad, looking down at them from the doorway. He held a wide-barrelled gun loosely in one hand and the end of a rope in the other. "Are you snooping around here again, Gimpy?" He laughed derisively. "I can't believe it. It would almost be worth staying at this stupid school to watch you getting into trouble for breaking into this lighthouse again."

Darrell eyed the gun warily. "What're you doing with the gun, Conrad? And what do you mean staying at the school? Mrs. Follett told me you were getting transferred."

Conrad laughed, a short, sharp sound without humour. "Follett's such a sucker. She believes anything she hears over the phone."

"So, you're not going to another school?"

"Are you kidding? I am never going back to school. I needed somewhere to stay for a while. This place was as good as any. Food's good, anyway. But now I'm outta here. One of my dad's friends is meeting me here this afternoon, and I won't have to put up with this stupid school or you jokers any longer."

Darrell eyed the steps. She could be down the stairs and out on the beach calling for help in a couple of seconds.

Brodie beat her to it. He started for the stairs. "Let's get out of here."

"Don't even think about it." Conrad gestured with the gun.

Brodie rolled his eyes. "You idiot! Quit acting like you're such a tough guy. That's not a pistol, it's a flare gun. Shoot it off in here and we all get burned, including you."

"I know it shoots flares, Sun, that's what I use it for. But if I shoot the dog, I'm not too worried about getting burned."

Brodie stopped on the step above the broken riser.

"Now get up here — all of you," Conrad snarled. "I'm going to lock the door to this room and catch my boat. By the time someone figures out where you are, I'll be long gone." He threw a piece of old rope at Kate. "Tie up that dog. I hate dogs."

Kate ignored the rope lying across her feet. Conrad reached down and grabbed Kate by the collar of her shirt. His eyes bored into Darrell's. "If you don't get up here right now, I'm going to shoot your dog on the count of three."

Darrell looked up and saw Kate close her eyes and clutch Delaney's collar. Darrell grabbed Brodie's hand, clenched her teeth, and stepped over the broken stair. The sound of a gunshot was swallowed by the roar of the wind that whirled them away.

"This is really bad, Darrell. What are we going to do?"

Darrell looked down at Conrad's face, pale and unconscious on the straw. She swirled the peppermint around in her mouth and tried to think, but her head was still spinning from the journey. "We've only got a few minutes before he wakes up," she whispered.

"Stupid idiot. Now he's going to find out *every-thing*. And he threatened to hurt Delaney, too." Kate looked as though she would like to kick the prone figure on the stable floor.

"Tie him up."

Darrell and Kate looked at Brodie, pulling himself onto his hands and knees. "Well, first give me one of those mints and then tie him up," Brodie corrected. He rubbed his eyes with one hand. Kate gave him a mint, and he got to his feet with a grimace.

Brodie pulled a piece of rough rope tangled around one of Kate's feet. Some of the colour returned to his face and he grinned a little.

"We'll use the rope Connie supplied, shall we?"

Conrad stirred. He rolled over on the straw and began to retch.

"Grab his hands, Kate."

"I don't know how to tie someone up." Kate looked frantic. She pulled one of Conrad's hands behind his back, but he yanked his hand back, rolled over, and was sick in the straw.

"Ugh!" Darrell grabbed Conrad by the back of his coat and helped Kate slide him away from the mess. "Brodie's right, Kate. This is the only thing we can do for now." After a few moments of struggle, Conrad lay on his side in the straw, his hands tied behind his back.

"What the hell are you doing?" he asked blearily. "Oh man — my head is killing me." He retched again.

"Better give him a mint, Kate," Brodie said.

"Ewww. No way. Besides, he wanted to hurt Delaney. I say we let him get over the nausea on his own."

Darrell took a mint from Kate's hand. "I don't know why I'm doing this," she said, and popped it in Conrad's mouth, "considering how you've managed to wreck everything."

Keeping well away from Conrad's mess on the straw, she turned to Brodie and Kate. "Okay. I know this changes everything, but I just have to see if I can find Leonardo. I can at least try to get his book back to him."

Kate looked anxious. "Are you going to try to talk to him about," she glanced at Conrad, "about the you-know-what?"

Darrell shrugged. "I don't know if I can even find Leonardo, and now you can't come with me in case *he* gets loose." She glared at Conrad. "It's probably safer for you to wait out here in the stable. You can watch this idiot to make sure he doesn't get into any trouble, and I'll get back as fast as I can."

"What's going to happen when we go back to Eagle Glen?" Kate sounded worried. "Conrad will tell, for sure."

Conrad's eyes darted from Darrell to Kate to Brodie and his mouth was clamped shut.

"And who is going to believe him?" Brodie's voice came out of the shadows. "He's already decided he's leaving the school. There's no one for him to tell."

In a sudden motion, Conrad kicked his legs and pushed himself along the floor toward the stable door. Brodie jumped beside him in a second and put a hand on his shoulder. Conrad strained his neck and his teeth clicked dangerously close to Brodie's fingers.

Kate shrieked. "Watch out, Brodie, he's trying to bite you." She ran over and sat on Conrad's legs.

"Get off!" He tried to swing his head forward to knock against her, but she used his momentum, flipped him onto his side, and wrapped her arms securely around his ankles. "This reminds me of something," she said, and flashed a brief smile. Darrell, remembering the events of the previous summer, smiled back, but her smile was strained.

"See what I mean?" She clutched the notebook. "I'll be back as soon as I can."

Brodie stuck his face into Conrad's. "Settle down for a minute and I'll tell you what's going on." He turned to Darrell. "Go find Leonardo. We'll be fine here."

Conrad bucked his legs, but Kate managed to hold on. "And be quick, okay?" she pleaded.

Darrell nodded and hobbled across the uneven dirt floor. "Quick as I can without my walking stick," she called and swung open the stable door. Delaney slipped out the door to lead the way.

The cold hit her with the force of a blow, and she struggled for a moment to close the stable door in the face of the stiff breeze. Darrell walked carefully along the icy garden path, mentally kicking herself for not thinking that there might be a change in the weather. Delaney's paws left black prints where his feet melted the frost. The air smelled of snow. A church bell rang in the distance, and suddenly it was like the cold air itself was vibrating as bells rang out all over the city, marking the noon hour.

Darrell tucked her hands into her long sleeves and hurried up the lane. Now that she knew the way, it didn't take long to find Leonardo's studio. The familiar marble lion still guarded the front, but she followed Delaney around back to the kitchen door.

She stepped into the kitchen and was surprised to find it empty and cold. Even the large wood-fired oven lay unlit and loaded with ashes. A single oil lamp glowed, and Darrell picked it up by the handle.

Delaney padded through the arched doorway and down the darkened hall.

"Wait for me, boy," Darrell whispered. This place was creepy when it was empty. *I'm just going to drop the book in the studio and head back to the stable.*

Delaney nosed a door open, and Darrell could see a wash of light flow into the hall. She swallowed and stepped into the room.

Two old men sat near a shuttered window, a single lamp on the table beside them. Both turned as Darrell entered the room. "Are you here to light the fire?" demanded one of the men.

Darrell held out the book. "I'm here to return something I — I found," she said in a low voice.

"Bring it here then, *bambina*."

Darrell stepped closer and gasped. "Cristofo!"

The old man laughed, and the other joined him, their voices creaking together in merriment. "You *do* look at bit like Cristofo, Giovanni," said the second old man, when he had regained enough breath to speak. "This is what age has brought us. We have become our grandfathers. "

Darrell turned and gazed into the eyes of Leonardo.

For the first time, he looked like the portraits she had seen of him in her research at the library. His beard was long and mingled with hair both grey and white. His hands resting on the table were still large, but were knotted with arthritis. Still smiling, he turned back to his friend. "Who is this young thing who knows your old grandfather?"

Giovanni shrugged. "Has Placida sent you to light the fires? It's about time — we will freeze in here before long."

Darrell nodded. It *was* very cold in the room. "I've come to bring you this," she said, moving aside a stack of half-painted canvasses and laying the notebook on the table. "And I can't stay long, but I will light the fire. It's too cold to sit here without one." She walked over to the fireplace, limping a little, and knelt to pile up wood and coal.

"She walks on a wooden leg," remarked Giovanni conversationally. "Why does that seem important?" He shook his head. "It seems I can remember nothing these days."

Leonardo tapped the table with a gnarled finger. "*I* remember a little girl who walked on a wooden leg long ago," he said quietly. "I wonder what became of her? I seem to recall she vanished like a dream — blown away like a wisp on the wind."

Darrell smiled to herself as she finished laying the fire. Using the stub of a candle she lit from the lamp, she soon had the tinder alight. She stood and walked back to the old men as warmth spread behind her and began to fill the room.

Giovanni was leafing through the notebook. He looked up at Darrell sharply, his blue eyes gleaming in the light of the fire.

"Where did you find this?"

"It appears to be one of my old notebooks," said Leonardo, reaching across the table. "Look! It is the one you gave me, with the letter 'L' on the cover."

"Uh — someone took it," Darrell muttered. "Someone took it and I found it and thought you might want it back."

Leonardo flipped the book back to Giovanni.

"What use would I have for it now?" The artist slammed his fist on the table. "I am an old man, destined to die as nothing more than a toymaker for a French king." He stood up and walked to the fire. Still tall, he leaned down to the flames to warm his hands. "I am given leave to see my old friend for but a day or two while the king dallies in *Firenze*, and then I must return to the life of a buffoon." He bent and tossed another log on the flames.

"Did you see the lion I made King Francis, Giovanni? Its mechanism allowed it to walk across the room, and inside its chest was a bouquet of flowers for the queen." He grabbed an iron poker and prodded the fire vigorously, his voice bitter. "Leonardo, maker of toy lions."

"You are the master, unsurpassed, without peer," said Giovanni quietly. "Look at all you have done in your long life, my friend."

"Do you know what it means?" Leonardo interrupted, his mouth twisted, "to be without peer?" He turned back to the table, and Darrell could see tears in his eyes.

Leonardo's voice was laden with emotion. "In my life I have wrapped myself in arrogance the way most men would wear a cloak. Today I am an old man, and I lie stripped bare of such things." He sighed deeply and returned to his chair. "You say I am without peer — but you are wrong," he said. "There are many who are great masters of their craft. Michelangelo. Raphael. My own teacher, Verrocchio. For most of my life I struggled to stand out among these other artists. I strove to put myself head and shoulders above them, but really I am no better or, please God, no worse than the rest."

Delaney curled in a brown ball, and Darrell sank onto a small stool near the fire. Leonardo grasped the hand of his friend across the table and his words poured out like a river of bitterness and defeat. Listening, Darrell felt as though she had no more presence in the room than the other ghosts populating Leonardo's memories.

"Giovanni, you know at times the painting was not enough. I had other windows open in my soul. I longed to find how the world worked, what made it so, and what more could be done. These notes," he gestured at the volume lying on the table between them, "these and my other notebooks captured my true love. My projects — the machines in all their mechanical glory can be found here. Here are my ideas of philosophy, theology, and more." He shook his head sadly. "And yet there is no one, save you, Giovanni, with whom I can share these innermost thoughts. When I attempt it, even the most enlightened mind reels. I have been lucky to escape charges of heresy." He slammed his fist on the table, causing the notebook to skip into the air and lightly skitter onto the floor.

Darrell's words tumbled out. "But what became of your secret project? I saw sketches in your notebook, but I could not understand any of it."

Leonardo stooped to pick up the volume and brandished it at her.

"No one understands my ideas — how to raise a sunken ship, how to power a machine to fly like a bird, how to travel to the great depths of the sea." He slumped into a chair, his brief burst of anger gone. He looked at Darrell and laughed a little. "My secret project was my biggest failure. I thought once there must be a way to harness time — ha!" He shook his head. "It cannot be done."

"But what if it can?" Darrell whispered.

He leaned over and cracked open a shutter, and grey light streamed into the room. "Look at me, *signorina*. This is what time accomplishes. It gnaws away at all beauty — at all life. What little of it I have slips away more quickly every day."

Leonardo held up one hand, fingers cruelly twisted with arthritis. "When you put your hand in the river, the water that you touch is the last of what has passed and the first of that which comes; so it is with present time."

He lifted one of the half-completed canvasses off the table. "I am losing my battle with time, but before I do, perhaps I may conquer that other great illusion."

"Illusion?" Darrell clenched her hands tightly in her lap. Disappointment and puzzlement struggled within her.

His raised his hand again and held it into the sunbeam streaming through the window. The light poured through the work-worn fingers and he flexed them as though trying to grasp the air. "Can't you guess, *signorina*? I seek to conquer the light. The very thing which illuminates all things has eluded me, and even after all these years I continue to struggle with its mysteries. And yet — if that great thief Time allows, perhaps I may still triumph." He shook his head and sighed.

Darrell gestured at the sketches and half-completed paintings strewn haphazardly across the table. They all depicted various studies of a woman's face. "Is this the *Mona Lisa*?" she asked quietly.

For a moment, Leonardo smiled into his beard, staring once more into the beam of light piercing the shadowy room from above. He spoke slowly. "I have never heard that name used to describe this particular lady. I know not yet who she will become. All that I know is that her portrait haunts me. Every day I spend a little time with her, and in the end, I hope that she will teach me the secret of light." He paused.

"I must work," he said, his voice suddenly sharp. "There is still much to do and my hours grow shorter each day." He pointed toward the door. "Send her away, Giovanni!"

Darrell stood and gathered her courage. "You sent me away once before, Leonardo, and I did what you said without question." She stepped nearer the table. "But you hold a secret locked within you — and I need to find the key!"

Darrell found she was shouting and had grasped the startled old man by the lapel of his collarless jacket. For an instant the room, and all within it, stood still.

"I know you care about this," she whispered. "You wrote it yourself: *Tempo, Spazio, Luce*. Time, Space, and Light. And I did not just blow away. I travelled through time. You saw me yourself."

Their eyes locked for an endless moment.

"I know who you are," he said, finally. "And I know from whence you come."

Darrell swallowed. "You do?"

Leonardo plucked her hand off his lapel and walked over to the table to stand beside his old friend. "You are the devil," he spat, "and you come from Hell."

His voice rose to a roar. "You give with one hand and take with the other. When I seek the truth of the secret contained in a beam of light across a woman's face, you offer me promises that mean nothing. Yes — I *have* seen you before. I remember as though it were yesterday when you were swept away in a whirl of wind. I was a young man, filled with ambition, and yes — with greed. I wanted all that your very presence implied. I wanted *time!*"

"So," Darrell interrupted the flow of the old man's words. Her face felt hot and she clenched her hands tightly at her side so Leonardo would not see them shake. "What did you do? Did you find out more?"

He shook his head. "No. After years of study, I could discover no more. And I convinced myself that you were but a dream — a dream come to haunt me like the ghost of my own failure. In the end," he swept a sketch off the table, "above all else, I am an artist. The answers I seek lie in light." His voice dropped and he smiled wryly. "There is no time left for me to study time."

Darrell felt her own anger and disappointment surge. "You said you could do it," she cried. "You said you could harness time, and I believed you! The secret of light is not important. It's the secret of *time* that I need. You are one of the greatest thinkers in history. How can you quit now?" She stepped forward, and one of the carefully carved toes of her wooden leg caught on the floor. She stumbled toward the table, but in a single smooth motion that belied his age, Giovanni stood and caught Darrell by the arms, steadying her.

She lifted her chin and felt the wetness of her own tears on her face. "There is much I could tell you," she said, her voice low and filled once again with the pain of her loss.

Leonardo remained facing the fire, but had pulled himself to his full height. "It is too late, *bambina*. I have turned my back on old failures. You must know," he met her eyes at last, "the secret you desire is *not* in my grasp." He stepped to the table and lifted the sketch depicting a quietly smiling woman's face into the sunbeam coursing through the window. "I think," he said, his tone firm, "that instead, I will seek the answer to a puzzle that it *is* within my power to solve."

Giovanni stepped to the door. He placed a hand on Delaney's head, and the dog's tail wagged like a gentle metronome.

Darrell followed slowly, limping a little, and stopped in the doorway. "There is so much more I need to know," she began.

"Well, my girl, there is much we all would know," Giovanni interrupted brusquely. "But we old men must content ourselves with that which we have. Within your grasp you have great riches Leonardo and I do not. Yours is the wealth of time. Do not waste this gift." With a firm hand on her arm, he drew Darrell into the dark hall and closed the door.

They walked through the hall and into the kitchen. The closing door had extinguished the last flame of hope within Darrell's heart. She slowly wiped away the traces of tears that felt like ice on her cheeks in the penetrating cold of the kitchen. An old woman clothed in black stood near the stove, feeding wood into a new fire she was kindling.

Giovanni's voice lightened. "Ah, Placida. You are here to create a masterpiece for our noon meal?"

The old lady made a rude noise as she expertly lit a lamp from the flame dancing on the tip of a tiny splinter of kindling. "I told you not to let the fire go out," she scolded. "Now I have much more work to do before I can feed you old fools." She pulled an iron ladle from a hook on the wall and looked disapprovingly down at the dog.

Giovanni smiled and put a hand on Darrell's arm. His eyes gleamed like sapphires in the light from the lamp. "I remember you now — you and your dog. And

I remember a strange story my grandfather once told. 'Treat her kindly, if you see her again,' he said to me. A whole lifetime ago."

He reached into a dark recess near the door and pulled out a heavy woollen shawl. "Please take this. Your journey may be cold. And take care in the streets, *cara*. These times bring great change, and trouble is often near." He clipped a tiny silver brooch onto the shawl, and with a last smile, he placed it in her hands.

Darrell clutched the shawl and looked into the kind eyes that reminded her so much of a young man from another century, another country. The questions welled within her but could not find a way to her lips. "I wish..." she whispered, at last.

"I do, too." As he smiled his farewell, she wrapped the shawl tightly around her shoulders and followed Delaney into the thin afternoon light.

Chapter Fifteen

Darrell made her way carefully along the lane leading to Verrocchio's stable. The sun had warmed the ground a little and most of the iciness had melted away. She thought about Giovanni's grandfather and sighed as she walked. The old notebook was back in its owner's hands, at least, but as it was for Leonardo, the secret of time still remained just beyond her reach.

Concentrating on trying not to slip, she was surprised as she turned the last corner to see a horse and cart pulled up behind Verrocchio's yard. She slipped behind a crumbling wall and peeked through the naked branches of a mulberry tree.

The door to the stable crashed open and a man came out carrying a large, squirming bundle over one shoulder. With some effort he thrust the bundle in the rear of the rickety old cart and jammed a board across the back.

"That's the last of them, Sal," called the man to the driver.

A blur of brown fur shot from behind the bush.

"Oy! Get off!" The man, startled, tried to aim a kick at the dog and then pulled himself onto the seat. The driver clicked to the horses, and the cart creaked slowly off down the lane. Delaney looked once over his shoulder at Darrell and trotted off after the cart, keeping pace behind the rear wheels.

Darrell, weak with fear, stumbled through the gate in the wall and over to the stable. The door hung loose on its hinges, and she stepped inside.

"Kate? Brodie?"

Nothing. Then Darrell heard a rustle coming from the tiny stall. A wooden crate that had stood on one end by the door was shattered in pieces all over the floor. Her heart in her throat, Darrell picked her way across the broken boards.

Kate was lying on the floor of the stall, her hands and feet bound with ropes and her eyes huge over the greasy rag stuffed into her mouth. At the sight of Darrell, she shrieked with fear and rage. The sound was muffled by the gag, and Darrell ran to free her.

"They've taken Brodie and Conrad," she said as soon as Darrell had pulled the filthy wad out of her mouth. "*Quick*, Darrell, untie me, we've got to go find them." She turned her head and began to spit the greasy taste out of her mouth.

"I'm trying! These knots are really tight." Darrell struggled to pull off the ropes but Kate cried out, so she went back to trying to untie them. "Tell me what happened."

Tears ran down Kate's face. "I'm not sure. Conrad was freaking out and he wouldn't stay still. We tried to explain the whole thing, but he wouldn't listen. I was tired of hanging onto his legs, and Brodie found some kind of twine inside the crate by the door, so we tied Conrad's feet. He started sliding across the floor, but we wouldn't let him move so he worked himself into a total tantrum."

Darrell loosened one of the knots at last and Kate's left hand came free. She wiped her tears away with the back of her wrist. "He didn't believe anything we said and he kept trying to get away. You were taking so long and we were worried, so we hauled Conrad over to that beam and propped him against it. Brodie tied him there so we could at least go somewhere quiet to make a plan about finding you, but that made Conrad really panic."

Kate pulled her hands away from Darrell. "Get my feet," she said, "and I'll work on getting this rope off my other wrist."

"Finish the story!" puffed Darrell, her fingers raw from tugging on the rough rope. "Maybe we can figure out where they've gone."

"Okay, okay. So Conrad started yelling. I got down on my knees beside him, trying to calm him down and talk some sense into him, and then I heard a thump. I heard a voice behind me say, 'This one'll do.' I didn't even have time to move or anything before someone grabbed me and pulled my arms back. It felt like they were going to break, Darrell, so I couldn't help screaming."

Kate stopped worrying at the knot and rubbed her other wrist. A tear rolled down off the tip of her nose.

"That's when they stuck the gag in my mouth." She shook her head. "I didn't have a chance to move. I feel like such an idiot. Some great black belt I am."

She wiped her nose with the back of her free hand. "Anyway, after they tied me, they put a big sack over Conrad and took him out of the stable. Brodie tried to help me, but they punched him and he fell down. That's the last I saw, 'cause they dragged me into the stall."

"Got it!" Darrell pulled the rope off and rubbed Kate's ankles briskly, trying to push down the panic that was threatening to overtake her. "Don't be so hard on yourself, Katie. You didn't have a chance with two men attacking you like that." She helped Kate to her feet and noticed a red mark on her neck where the skin was bruised and torn. "What's that?"

The tears welled in Kate's eyes again. "He bit me," she said quietly. "He told the old man he'd caught himself a nice little chicken and he wanted to take me with him. His breath was so gross, Darrell, and I thought I was going to be sick, but I knew I'd choke to death with the rag in my mouth, so I just closed my eyes and hoped he'd go away. The old guy yelled at him to leave me because he'd made his quota — whatever that meant — and they had to go collect their gold at the marketplace. It must have made him mad, because he bit me and then threw me down in the straw."

"Oh, Kate, I'm so sorry." Darrell hugged her friend tightly. "We'd better get out of here fast." She jumped up. "I'm going to need a crutch or some kind of walking stick or I'll never be able to walk with any speed at all."

"You can hang on to me. We don't have time to look for a crutch." Kate looked around. "Where's Delaney?"

"He followed the cart. They were heading down the lane. If we can find Delaney, I bet we can find Brodie and Conrad."

They hurried out of the stable, and Darrell looked around frantically. She noticed for the first time that Verrocchio's old house was tightly boarded. The kitchen garden was a mass of dead weeds, and the plaster surface of the building was cracked and stained. There was no sign of the cart.

"It's hard to believe no one lives there anymore," she said as they hurried along the road.

"Did you get the book back to Leonardo?" said Kate.

"Yeah."

"And?"

Darrell stared at the ground. "He doesn't have any more information on time machines than I do," she said quietly. "And he's grown very old now. I think I'm back to square one."

Kate gave her arm a sympathetic squeeze as they hurried off. The road widened and began to fill with more passers-by. The surface changed from dirt to cobbles and then to brick, becoming progressively easier for Darrell to walk upon. They stepped out into the square and stopped in shock.

The entire *Piazza del Duomo* was filled with stalls. Merchants of every description were selling their wares to shoppers who strolled along the streets.

"None of this was here the last time," breathed Darrell. "It must be market day."

"Just like our Renaissance fair," said Kate. "But it's jammed with people. How're we ever going to find the guys?"

"We need to find Delaney. He'll know we're looking for him." Darrell looked critically at the nearest stall. "We sure got the details wrong," she muttered. "This doesn't looks like our fair at all."

Most of the stalls were little more than a stack of wooden crates, some tilting perilously. There wasn't a single colourful tent in sight, and the air was ripe with the smell of animals alive and dead. In one stall, a woman had erected an enormous loom and was weaving a coarse cloth as her daughters sold squares of fabric. At the next spot, a woman sold brightly tinted yarns while another sat behind, spinning greasy sheep's wool into long, grey strands.

Dogs ran untended through the market, chasing cats and stealing food, but there was no sign of Delaney.

Stalls with live chickens for sale stood next to those selling pigeons, ducks, and other fowl already roasted and ready for eating. There were spiced wines, mead, and sweet waters. Darrell and Kate dodged through the shoppers and the shopkeepers as best they could.

A few men in uniform sat around low tables drinking ale near a barn with a bugle nailed over the door. Beside the makeshift pub a man thrust a small dagger into Kate's hand. "Try this blade, *signorina*. It'll keep ye safe on a dark night." Kate hurriedly dropped the knife back onto the crude countertop the man had created with an irregular slice of canvas laid across a board. Darrell shook her head firmly at a second man brandishing a large shield. "Your family crest can be painted on the front," he called to their retreating backs.

Some children ran and played in the marketplace, but most seemed to be working in the stalls with their parents. Darrell watched one child milking a goat tied to the corner of the family's stall. He poured half of the creamy contents into an earthen jar for his mother and then drank the rest right out of the small pail.

There were several stalls featuring clay mugs and dishes and many with beads and other tiny decorations for sewing onto clothes and hats. A shoemaker fitted leather around a lady's foot in preparation for making slippers, and one tiny girl stood watch over a table laden with small wooden flutes.

Darrell stopped in front of a stall holding pieces of finely wrought jewellery. She unclipped the silver brooch from her shawl. "Will you buy this?"

The woman behind the counter looked her over carefully. "Did you steal it?" she asked brusquely.

Darrell shook her head. "I've — I've had a bit of a family emergency and I have to sell it."

The woman raised an eyebrow skeptically. "It is a lovely piece…" She hesitated a moment and then slid a few coins across the rough wooden counter. Darrell scooped up the copper pieces and handed a couple to Kate.

"I'm going to keep looking around here. Can you go buy some water and maybe a bit of bread? We may need some food before this is over."

Kate nodded. "I'll meet you over at that bench. This will only take a minute, then we can keep looking."

While Kate bought the bread and water, Darrell walked over and sat on a small stone bench near the cathedral. By her reckoning, they had made a complete circle of the marketplace. Where else could they look?

Kate ran up and handed Darrell the bread. She had a water skin slung around one shoulder. "They don't seem to have any plain water," she said, panting a little. "I bought this sweet water — I think it has honey in it." She made a face. "They took all the money, Darrell. I hope it's okay."

"Don't worry about it, I've still got a coin left. I hope we can find the guys and get out of here soon." She reached down and rubbed her right knee. "I'm sorry, Kate. My leg is so sore, I just have to rest for a minute."

Kate's face was pale with worry. "This is a huge city, Darrell. If they're not near this marketplace, we may never find them."

Darrell's stomach was clenched in a tight knot. "We have to watch for Delaney. He's our only hope." Kate sat down and Darrell clutched her sleeve. "Can you remember anything else the man said?"

"Just that he could collect his gold at the market. Why would he get gold for Brodie and Conrad? They didn't have slaves during the Renaissance, did they?"

"I don't know! I don't remember reading about slaves, but why else would you be able to sell..." She paused. Understanding washed over her and she stood up and hurried back the way they had come.

"What is it, Darrell?" Kate caught up and took Darrell's arm to help her negotiate a rough section of cobbles.

"It's got to be the soldiers, Kate. When I did my research, I read about the war between France and Italy during the fourteenth and fifteenth centuries." She stopped speaking as she spotted the soldiers still seated outside the barn and began to work her way between two stalls nearby. A woman with a tray of pewter buttons eyed her warily as Darrell smiled apologetically and squeezed past, towing Kate by the arm. A dark lane ran behind the stalls, and filthy brown water trickled along a ditch. The smell of drains and farm animals seemed even worse, and the lane was almost deserted apart from a dirty brown dog curled against the side of a barn. At the sight of them, the dog leaped up.

"Delaney!" A smudge of muddy brown shot toward them, and Darrell almost cried with relief as he pushed his head into her hands. She scurried across the cobbles to peek through a broken board in the barn.

"Can you see them?" whispered Kate.

"I can't tell — it's too dark. But they've got to be in there, 'cause Delaney's here." She leaned against the wall of the barn. "I'm going in," she said.

"Are you crazy? You are *not* going in! We've got to find another way."

Darrell put her hands on Kate's arms. "Listen. We need to find Brodie and Conrad before the soldiers take them away for good. I have to see if they're inside. You have two good legs, Kate. If they catch me, you can run and get Leonardo and Giovanni."

"Darrell, you told me yourself they are old men now. They don't even know me. How can they help us?"

Darrell took a deep breath. "Let's hope we don't need them, then." She crept around the corner and saw a small opening that may have once been a window. She beckoned to Kate. "Give me a lift, here!"

Darrell grabbed the sill with both hands and boosted herself by stepping on Kate's bent knee. She slipped and tumbled through the opening, rolling to a mercifully soft landing against a bale of hay.

"Are you okay, Darrell?" whispered Kate.

"Shhh! I'm fine." Darrell struggled to right herself in the grey light of the barn. She could see the last light of evening streaming in from a window high above, and realized she had fallen into a stall in the back corner. She turned to find a large, black cow chewing a mouthful of the very hay she had landed on. Darrell looked down to see she had narrowly avoided covering her dress in the remains of the hay — after the cow had processed it. A large brown puddle congealed behind the cow.

"Oh — yuck!" She hurriedly stepped over to the edge of the stall.

"Who's that?" A voice came from just outside the stall. Darrell peeked out to see Conrad, trussed like a Christmas turkey, leaning awkwardly against a bale of hay. On one side of him was a young man in a blue cloak and on the other side Brodie lay crumpled in the straw.

"Shhh. It's me, Conrad. I'm trying to get you guys out of here, so be quiet, okay?"

Conrad nodded, for once not frowning at the very sight of her. The young man beside him looked on with interest. Darrell crept out of the stall over to Brodie.

He was curled on the floor near one wall of the barn. He, too, had been bound tightly with coarse ropes, and she could see where his shirt had been torn. Blood oozed from his lower lip, and his eyes, only half-open, were dazed.

"Brodie — Brodie. Wake up." Darrell hissed in his ear and shook him, but his head lolled to one side. "Oh — oh, please, Brodie, please wake up."

Brodie blinked at Darrell. "Just need a little more sleep..." he mumbled. "Be better in the morning..."

"His eyes opened." Conrad's whisper carried across from where he was sitting. "Try some water."

"I can't pour water down his throat. He's unconscious; I might drown him!"

"Not down his throat, you idiot. There's a barrel of water over there by the door. Wet a rag and wipe his face."

Darrell glanced at Conrad. "Okay, okay, I get it."

Staying in the shadows, she crept around the walls to the water barrel near the door. It was clearly used for watering the animals and had a great deal of straw floating on top. She didn't want to guess what else might be found in the murky depths. Wetting a stiff scrap of cloth that hung on a nail, she returned to her spot beside Brodie.

He opened his eyes as she wrung the excess water out of the filthy rag.

"Don't put that repulsive thing near my face," he croaked.

"Brodie!" Darrell's heart lifted.

He winced. "Shhh," he muttered weakly. "I'm happy to see you, too, but could you keep it down? My head is killing me."

Darrell lifted his head so his neck was supported by a balled-up piece of sacking. "I'm so glad you're okay," she whispered. "Just wait a minute." She hurried back into the tiny stall to see Kate's worried face peering through the old window.

"I've found them. Can you pass me the water?"

Kate beamed and hurled the skin through the window. Her face disappeared and Darrell could hear her praising Delaney. Darrell gave the broad back of the cow a quick rub and crept out of the stall.

"Here, try a sip of this. It's probably warm, but at least it's clean."

Brodie managed to take a sip through cracked lips, then lay back once more on the sacking.

"Oh, man, I feel really crummy," he muttered. Darrell nodded sympathetically.

"Try some more water. And then take one of these." She gave him a peppermint from her pocket.

Brodie grinned a little. "Well, I'd rather have a Tylenol, but this will have to do." Darrell smiled, relieved, and went to work on the ropes binding his hands.

"Hey, get over here and untie me," Conrad hissed.

"Wait a minute, Conrad. I've got to make sure Brodie is okay." Darrell struggled to untie the knots cutting deeply into Brodie's wrists.

"He's talking, isn't he? The guy kicked me in the head, too, y'know."

"Ssst!" The young man in the blue cloak jerked his head towards the stall at the back. "Get back into the byre! Someone is coming."

Darrell grabbed the water skin and the rag and scurried back to the stall. Inside, the cow lowed gently in greeting. Darrell rubbed the broad back absently and slid into the darkest corner.

"I see yer awake, *feiglio de cagne*." Darrell could hear heels click on the floor of the barn. "It's not long now before the wagon arrives. You'll be at the front in three days and have a chance to show yerselves as men and not the dogs ye seem to be, and I'll have a few more pieces of gold in my pocket."

Darrell winced at the sound of a boot meeting flesh. From the stream of vitriolic Italian, she guessed the young man in the blue cloak had been the target.

The tormentor laughed. "Yer tongue's working, anyway. Primo! Draw me another mug of your best ale. These three will keep for an hour more." The light dimmed as he swung the door shut, and Darrell heard the board that barred the door clunk into place. She counted to twenty before creeping back into the barn.

"Untie me first," ordered Conrad, "then I'll help you undo Brodie." Darrell glared at him and turned again to the ropes binding Brodie's wrists.

"*Signorina.*" The young man in the blue cloak smiled at Darrell, though she could see a fresh line of blood running around his lips. "I have a dagger in my right boot," he whispered. "My greatest shame is I did not have time to draw it to save myself from these *porco diablo* thieves of men."

Darrell crawled over through the straw and found the small blade at once.

The young man gestured with his head. "Cut your friend free first. You will see, unlike the *feigli de cagne* who brought us here, I am an honourable man."

With the sharp knife, Darrell had Brodie free in seconds. As he rubbed his sore wrists and ankles, Darrell turned her attention to the young man.

"What's your name?" she whispered, as she sawed through the rope around his wrists.

"My name is Remo Giancarli, and I owe you my life." The ropes fell away, and before Darrell could react, he grabbed her face and planted a kiss on each cheek.

"You're welcome," she said, startled.

"Now, once we free your other friend, I will take you to a place of sanctuary where we may hide safely until we can send word to your family." Grimacing as he got to his feet, he hobbled over to help Brodie up.

"Thank you. That would be wonderful!" Darrell began cutting the rope off Conrad's ankles.

"It's about time. And make sure you're careful with that thing!" Conrad's words showed traces of his usual bluster, but his face was drawn with anxiety. Darrell remembered her own shock and fear during her initial journey through time, and for a moment she felt something akin to pity for him. She paused.

"Conrad, I don't have time to explain anything right now. Promise me you'll do what you're told until we can get you back to the lighthouse."

"Listen — I don't even want to know. I'm speaking a different language, I'm wearing some kinda fruitcake clothes, a jerk put a bag over my head and kidnapped me — man, this is like my worst nightmare."

Darrell was unconvinced. "Just do what we tell you and it should be okay." Conrad nodded. She cut the final bonds at his wrist and handed the knife back to Remo.

Kate was positively beaming with relief as she helped them through the window. All three boys staggered a little as they hurried away from the back of the barn. Delaney capered joyfully around Brodie, but Darrell noticed he kept carefully clear of Conrad.

The sun had fallen low in the sky and the cold deepened, wrapping itself around the corners of the buildings, filling the shade and creeping under collars and into sleeves. After the warmth of the cow barn, the wind bit deeply. Without a word, Remo beckoned, and they followed him as he moved through the growing shadows of the dusk. They wove their way along lanes and around buildings, avoiding the marketplace entirely. Darrell looked through the waning light to see the dome of the cathedral emerging into the sky above the narrow street.

"The *Duomo*?"

Remo nodded. "My uncle is one of the priests. But we must go the back way — there is a secret door."

Darrell's leg throbbed as she limped along beside Kate. Brodie was also looking a little unsteady on his feet, so it was several more long moments before Remo knocked on a wall at the back of the cathedral. Tiny cracks appeared in the wall along the lines of the ornate fretwork, and it opened as though on hinges. A hooded figure stood in the shadows.

Remo whispered a few words then turned and nodded. The figure stepped aside and they all filed through the tiny secret door, Delaney following at the rear.

Darrell looked around in the cramped entry, lit by a single candle that flickered and danced in a sconce on the wall above. The monk removed his hood and his tonsured head gleamed in the candlelight.

"I am Brother Raul," he said. "Follow me." He turned to Darrell and his voice was curt. "You must keep that dog quiet. Such beasts are not permitted to roam the halls of this cathedral." Darrell, her hand on Delaney's head, nodded mutely.

The monk removed the candle from the sconce and carried it as they followed in a silent train, single file down a narrow corridor redolent with beeswax and incense. The monk wore a white, ankle-length habit, hooded in black. The rough wool of the tunic seemed ghostly in the candlelight as he made his way, swift and silent, along the darkened passage. A left turn took them down a narrow, winding flight of steps and then along another confined hall, this one damp and clammy with an earthen floor. Brother Raul stopped abruptly and pulled open a heavy wooden door with an iron handle.

"Brother Constantine's chamber," he said quietly.

Inside the small room he used his candle to light another sitting on a tiny desk against a wall. The light flickered to reveal a Spartan room furnished only with a cot in one corner, a single chair, and the tiny desk. Two hooks on the wall held a long robe of rough, white wool and a short, black cape. A man knelt beside the bed, his murmured prayer interrupted, and his face turned up to them in surprise.

"Remo!" He leaped to his feet. "What brings you here?"

Brother Raul replaced his hood and nodded, closing the door as he left.

"Uncle Tino, I was stolen this afternoon by men seeking to sell me into armed service." He gestured at the others. "The three of us were taken to the marketplace to be transferred to the battlefront by bondsmen." He grinned at Darrell and his teeth flashed briefly in the light of the candle. "These girls are our rescuers."

Brother Constantine clasped Darrell's hands briefly and then Kate's before looking back at his nephew. "Your brother?"

"He is safe at home. The black marketeers caught me when I was checking out the barns for a new horse. They called me a deserter, took my money, and threw me in their cart."

Brother Constantine shook his head. "I can't wait to hear what your mama will say about this," he muttered and shook his nephew gently by the arm. "You should never go through the barns without your father, Remo. These times are not safe, even for those of noble blood. You know that!"

Remo nodded.

The monk's face was worried. "I must make my way to the street to see if there is news of your disappearance. If they label you a deserter, a whole detachment could be brought in to search. You may have to hide here for some time until the interest dies down and we can safely get you back to your home. I will be but a few moments." With quick, deft movements he donned his white robe, belting it with a leather strap. He tucked his rosary into his belt and pulled the cowl over his head before slipping out the door.

Conrad sat down on the bed and bounced a little. "Nice room," he said sarcastically. "I've seen jail cells that are more comfortable than this."

"The monks of this order seek simplicity," whispered Remo. "They have very plain clothes and food and put their strength into serving God."

"Yeah, and all their money, too, from the looks of it. Did you see the marble this place is covered in? And the gold stuff everywhere? Somebody's got a lot of coin to throw around."

"The Cathedral of Santa Maria del Fiore is still being built," said Remo, raising a haughty eyebrow. "My uncle is very privileged to be one of the Dominican order who are God's servants here. This cathedral is a testament to the talents of our artists and is dedicated to the glory of the mother of the saviour."

He turned to Darrell. "I have to thank you again for your help, *signorina*. We will stay here in the old section of the cathedral until my father arrives, and then I will make my way home under the cover of darkness. Do you have a way to return to your homes in safety?"

Darrell nodded. "I think so. We have only a few streets to travel and I know the way, as long as we don't meet those — did you call them — bondsmen?"

Remo nodded. "They steal boys and young men off the streets and sell them to some of the less law-abiding commanders at the battle front. Usually they are the poor and the no-account so they are not missed. There is always a need for more soldiers for the war, and this form of conscription is very common."

Kate spoke. "Why wouldn't they be missed? You may be of noble blood, Remo, but not everyone who is poor is of no account. Those boys and men must all have families somewhere, too."

Remo nodded, though he still looked defiant. "Perhaps. But if I go to the army, I will go as an officer. My father will see to that."

Kate raised her eyebrows at Darrell but said nothing.

"One of the commanders came into the barn before you got there, Darrell. He's the one who smacked me in the face," said Brodie.

"What happened?"

Brodie sat on the floor by the bed and stroked Delaney, who lay curled beside him. "Well, first they hauled us out of the cart and threw us into the barn. They left the sack over Conrad's head but for some reason they took mine off. I was feeling pretty sore from getting punched, but other than that I was okay. Then this new guy came in and yelled, 'Soldier, get to your feet and stand at attention.' My head was still spinning and so he yelled at me again."

Brodie rubbed his wrists, still bearing red weals from the ropes. "So I said I'd heard him but didn't think he'd really meant it. 'Let me assure you, I meant every word. On your *feet*!' He screamed so loud the veins stood out on his temples. I had to find a way to stand up with my hands and feet tied. I don't think he expected me to be about a foot taller than him, so his eyes bulged." He shook his head at the memory.

"He stomped back and forth in front of me. 'Yer a fine, tall young whelp, it's clear,' he said. 'Skinny, but the skinny ones make smaller targets.' Right about then another guy came in with Remo and dumped him on the straw."

Conrad laughed from his spot on the bed.

Brodie glared at him. "What's so funny?"

"Tell them about the musket."

Brodie narrowed his eyes. "If you think it's so funny, you tell it," he said.

"Okay, I will." Conrad leaned forward, his hands on his knees. "The guy yelling at Brodie came over to me and pulled the sack off my head and hauled me to my feet. My legs had gone numb from the ropes, so I fell. The guy tried to give me a boot in the ribs, but he got my arm instead so it didn't hurt so bad. Then he yelled at Brodie again."

Conrad stood, miming the soldier talking to Brodie. "'Can you shoot a matchlock, ya beanpole?' And Mr. Polite over there starts to stammer and stutter. 'A — a matchlock, sir?' he says." Conrad chuckled again. "So the soldier roars: 'Y've quite clearly outgrown yer brains, I can see. A *musket*.' And then he waves this stupid gun that looked like some kid's homemade toy in Brodie's face."

"That is no toy. It is the latest weapon in use by our armies. A true musketeer can load and shoot a matchlock three times in under a minute," Remo interrupted hotly.

Conrad narrowed his eyes, and his face looked thoughtful. After a moment he shook his head and continued as if coming out of a daze. "The soldier's face was beet red and he was so mad his hands were shaking. 'Are ye deaf now, too, ye lousy turnip?'"

Conrad warmed again to his story and smirked at Brodie. "So Mr. Beanpole answers 'No sir,' in his namby-pamby voice. 'I'm not deaf. But I think you've mistaken me for someone else.'" Conrad sat down on the cot. "That's when the soldier got mad. He smacked Brodie in the face with the gun and knocked him down. I kept my mouth shut," Conrad pointed a finger at Brodie, "the way *you* should have done in the first place — and the guy swore at us and ran outside. I could hear him out there yelling at somebody else."

The scrape of a heel in the hall made Conrad blanch and fall silent. The door to the chamber snicked open and Brother Constantine slipped inside.

Remo stood up. "What news?"

"The army is abroad, Remo." His uncle sighed. "They are searching the area, but should move on soon. They have other deserters to find, thank God." He looked at Darrell, his eyes reflecting deep sadness and compassion. "So many men and boys sent to die on fields of battle far from their homes. I do not want my nephew to be among them." He took Remo by the arm. "I have sent word to your father to send a carriage. You cannot travel securely without an escort."

Remo nodded. "Thank you, Uncle. We are all in your debt."

"While you are in the cathedral, you have sanctuary, and we can safely walk upstairs. I have arranged to meet the carriage at the Door of the Canonici on the south side of the building. Follow me, but please, do not speak. After sundown we maintain complete silence."

He replaced his cowl over his head and, grasping the candle holder, led the way out into the hall. They followed what seemed to be a maze of tunnels through dark halls smelling of damp. At last they came to a flight of unadorned wooden steps and began to climb. Darrell's leg was tired and sore, but she followed the group closely, more worried about getting left behind than about her sore leg. Delaney padded at her side, head high and eyes alert.

They emerged into the centre nave of the cathedral and headed for the south door. Apart from a few distant spots of light, the velvet dark enclosed them. Darrell could feel the majesty of the great building, and the volume of the silence was like a crescendo around her. Arches supported by soaring pillars took wing into the darkness of ceilings far above. The air was suffused with the heavy smell of incense, and in the main hall a few torches burned in wall sconces to light their way. The cathedral formed the shape of an enormous cross, and Darrell knew one end was crowned with the huge dome she had seen from outside.

She stopped for a moment beside a clock illuminated by a nearby torch on the inner façade. "Look!" she whispered and elbowed Kate. Brother Constantine raised a warning hand, but paused for a moment, allowing Darrell the chance for a closer glimpse.

The clockwork echoed in the vast silence, and Darrell watched the lone hand slide backwards to indicate the passage of a single moment in time. The face of the clock bore twenty-four roman numerals beginning at the bottom and circling counter-clockwise. Remo's uncle moved on to the door and Darrell, with a last look at the strange clock, was forced to follow.

A carriage clattered to a stop outside the door, and the monk ruffled the hair of his nephew and waved a silent goodbye to the other travellers as they climbed on board. Remo clapped a felt hat on his head and swung into the driver's seat next to the driver. Darrell could hear the conversation from the open seat rise and fall over the clop of the horse's hoofs as they travelled down the road to the Giancarli family home. Cold air blew through the unglazed windows of the carriage.

Narrowing her eyes against the wind, Darrell leaned her head out the window and was just able to see Delaney jogging at a comfortable pace behind the carriage. She spied a small group of soldiers stopped outside what looked like an inn, but not a single head lifted to view the carriage as it passed, intent instead on the warmth and revelry inside.

"There's Verrocchio's stable," whispered Kate as the carriage jolted along the rutted lane. "Darrell — I'm so sorry you couldn't find the secret of time."

Darrell smiled a little. "I've just been thinking about that. One good thing happened, though."

Kate looked quizzical.

"After all those years of hating girls, it was a woman who taught Leonardo the secret he most wanted to learn." She leaned out the open window of the carriage and tugged on Remo's shoe. A moment later, his face appeared through the window.

"Could you please ask your driver to stop here? We are very near our — our home."

Remo nodded and his face disappeared. The horses slowed and the driver appeared at the carriage door. Darrell realized from his fine clothes and similar appearance that she must be looking at Remo's father.

He glanced over at the boarded windows of Verrocchio's old home. "My son has just informed me of the peril you saved him from this day. I would take you to our home and provide you with safe lodging before you return to your family. This surely cannot be where you stay?"

Darrell took his proffered hand and stepped gingerly out of the carriage. "Oh — thank you sir, but we will be fine. Our, uh — our carriage is housed in the stable here, and we will be quite safe on our trip home."

Remo's father bowed. "As you wish. Remember, however, a life-debt is owed you by the Giancarli family of *Firenze*. We will never forget your aid to our son."

Darrell nodded and stepped quickly away in case Remo's father offered his thanks in the same manner as his son, but was instead rewarded with a gallant bow.

"I don't hear anybody thanking me," said Conrad, as they walked over to the stable. "I coulda taken off and saved myself, but I stuck around to make sure you guys were okay."

Kate rolled her eyes as the carriage clattered off into the night. "Let's just get home, all right? This has been one long day I will never forget." She opened the door to the stable and found her wrist suddenly clasped in an iron grip.

"Here she is, Salvatore. My sweet little chicken's come home to her coop."

CHAPTER SIXTEEN

Darrell stood, her leg trembling with exhaustion, and clutched Kate's hand as they stared down the barrel of the gun wielded by the man known as Salvatore. He looked far too old for this line of work, and a shiny white scar scored his face from eye to chin.

"Luck has smiled upon us, Vito, after the small problem of this afternoon," he said softly, and set the oil lamp he held on a wooden crate. Conrad and Brodie stood under the watchful eye of Vito, whom Darrell recognized as the man she had seen throwing one of the boys into the back of the cart earlier that day. She saw a glance pass from Brodie to Conrad.

"What are you going to do with us?" she asked, stalling.

"Oh, your friends over there will go back to the commander. I'm sure he'll be delighted to see them again. And as for you, pretty girls…"

A creak of a hinge silenced him and all turned to the door. A skinny brown shape wriggled though the doorway.

Darrell's breath caught in her throat. "Delaney!"

Both guns turn to point at the dog, and in that instant, Brodie leaped. He landed squarely on the back of Vito and squashed him flat. The musket flew out of his hand.

Brodie yelled, "Grab the gun!" and Conrad was on it in an instant, aiming it straight at Salvatore. Delaney barked and scampered up the stairs to stand on the edge of the tiny hayloft.

Salvatore grinned, showing the blackened stumps of his teeth. "It all comes down now to who best can aim," he said, and he tucked the weapon more firmly under his arm and pointed it straight at Conrad.

"I disagree," said Conrad, with a strange smile. "I believe we have a situation here that we can both profit from, Mr. Salvatore, *sir*." He gestured with his musket. "You can have these three in exchange for the pouch of gold you have hanging on your belt. You can sell 'em and get your money back in no time flat. Get them out of here, and I'll look after myself."

Darrell was stunned. "You've got to be kidding, Conrad," she said. "What are you thinking?" She glanced sideways and saw a look of disgust on Brodie's face.

"It's not much of a choice, is it, Gimp? Let's see — do I get hauled off to fight in a war in whatever godforsaken century we're in, or do I grab the gold and take my time finding my merry way back to Eagle Glen?"

"You don't know the way," Kate blurted, a mixture of anger and despair in her voice.

"Hey, I know the entrance is around here somewhere, 'cause this is where you were all heading. I'm not in any hurry. I'll find it."

Keeping the musket at point-blank aim, he shuffled over to the steps leading to the tiny hayloft. "I tell the good professor a long, sad story about the three of you stealing a boat for a joyride and how I nobly tried to stop you." He laughed. "Not that she'll believe my noble impulses, but there won't be anyone around to contradict me, will there?" He jerked his head at Salvatore. "Do we have a deal?"

Behind Conrad's back, Brodie shifted his position on Vito's legs. One of Vito's arms was trapped beneath him, and Brodie twisted the other arm high on his back to hold him. Darrell watched as Brodie put his free hand on the dagger in the scabbard at Vito's waist.

Salvatore shrugged. "I don't think I want to give up my gold," he said, and put his finger on the trigger.

Brodie pulled the dagger out of the scabbard.

"Watch him, Sal!" Vito wailed. Conrad looked at Vito and Salvatore's musket exploded.

Darrell saw Conrad stagger off the step as a red spray flowered from one arm. His own musket fired and shot wild, hitting the oil lamp standing on the crate near the door. The darkness filling the small stable exploded into light as flames raced across the floor and straight up the walls of the old building. Salvatore, splashed with oil from the lamp, was suddenly ablaze and ran like a screaming human torch straight into the arms of Vito, who flung him through the door and rolled him on the icy ground outside to smother the flames.

Darrell had a final sight of Salvatore, his clothes smoking as he lay stunned on the ground outside, while Vito leaped back through the smouldering door to drag Conrad along the ground and out of the stable.

In an instant, Darrell watched her whole world burst into flame.

When she opened her eyes, the brilliance that had seared them with its hellish beauty was gone, and her vision was obscured as though by a thick, grey blanket. Around her was an orchestra of fire; the roar of flame, the crack of collapsing timbers, and the explosive popping of wood assaulted her, and she placed her hands over her ears to protect them from the sudden cacophony. The blanket lifted and at her feet she watched the straw change form in an instant, from yellowed grass to brilliant lines of red fire to incinerated ash.

The heat on her face was terrible — so intense that she felt her skin might melt. And there was nothing left to breathe; the fire greedily swallowed the air and left only ash that filled her mouth and adhered to her tongue. She closed her eyes and waited to be consumed.

Instead she felt a yank on her arm and she fell to the side, barking her shin painfully. The shock of the pain in her leg cleared her thoughts enough to stumble forward. Her arm felt like it was being pulled out of the socket and her groping hand found a scrap of fabric and clutched at it like she was drowning. Something impossibly cold touched her cheek and she fell forward as any last hope of breath was taken by a wind that whirled her away.

CHAPTER SEVENTEEN

Darrell sat on a log half-buried in sand and stared out at the water, thinking. It felt like this was the first moment she had been alone and quiet for months. Delaney gave his open-mouthed, tongue-lolling smile, and she ruffled the rich fur at his neck, as golden as if it had always been that way.

At the far end of the beach to the north, a group of boulders stood like ancient fallen soldiers tumbled into the surf. Behind them was a crevice in the rock face of the cliff curving out to meet the sea. And inside the crevice was the cave where everything had started. But she couldn't think of that now.

"We need a little time to ourselves, right buddy?"

His tail thumped once, and he lay his heavy head on her knee. Her fingers curling in the fur at his neck, she turned to look at the charred remains of the lighthouse. She still felt stunned when she looked at it — the physical evidence of how badly she had managed to mess up so many lives, most especially her own.

Kate was finally asleep, after spending the night plagued by nightmares. Brodie was blue along one side of his rib cage from being kicked. And Conrad?

Where was Conrad?

Was he alive? Was he dead? She would never know, because the only way to get him back was closed, burned to the ground, gone forever. The old lighthouse was gone, no longer a portal to anyone but rats sheltering from the sea spray. At the very tip of the rock promontory, a brand new light on a high cement pillar towered above the jumble of charred wood and shattered concrete.

Gravel crunched behind her, and she looked around to see Brodie making his way across the rocky shore. Delaney stretched and yawned, and then strolled over to escort Brodie to her spot on the sand.

"Mind if I pull up a piece of log?"

"Hey, if you're crazy enough to come out here in the cold, you're welcome to sit down."

He winced a little as he sat next to her on the damp wood.

"Are you okay?" she asked anxiously. The chill of the misty air seemed to wrap itself around her heart.

"It's just a bruise," he replied, and changed the subject. "Feels like it's going to snow soon," he said, "but it'll probably be raining again here when we get back in January."

"Yep," said Darrell, but the thought of coming back to the school and trying to resume a normal life was too much. She put her face into her hands.

He touched her wrist gently. "How are *you* feeling?"

She lifted her head abruptly and looked him straight in the eyes. "I just dragged my friends through an inferno," she said bitterly. "One can't sleep for screaming nightmares and the other looks like he broke a rib. And on top of that, I managed to burn someone else up in a fire that actually took place around five hundred years ago."

She clenched her hands so tightly that her fingernails dug into the flesh of her palms. "But me? Not even a scratch. I can't believe you want to have anything to do with me after all that's happened, Brodie." Her eyes stung with unshed tears.

He squeezed her hand gently and glanced up at the new beacon, hard to see in the misty afternoon light.

"They sure got that thing up fast," he said.

Darrell didn't reply, but sat and stared at the blackened ruins of the old lighthouse. "D'you think he could be there, under all the rubble?" she asked, her voice a bare whisper above the sound of the surf.

"If he is, it's for the best," Brodie said, his tone hard. "He tried to sell us out, Darrell. He wanted to leave us behind and make a little cash in the process. He nearly killed us all."

"Instead, we've lost *him*. He's gone. And the portal is gone — closed forever."

"He deserved it." A little awkwardly, he reached over and patted her arm. "Professor Tooth thinks he ran away."

Darrell gave a short, humourless laugh. "Yeah. Just a little further away than anyone expected."

Brodie shrugged. "He did. He made his own choices, Darrell."

She sighed. "He was so much like Leonardo, you know."

"Conrad? You can't be serious."

Darrell traced a pattern in the sand with a bit of stick. "Neither of them had very loving families. I think they both just needed a little more attention."

Brodie laughed. "That just sounds like pop psychology, Darrell. Leonardo was one of the greatest artists of all time. Conrad was just a loser."

"Paris didn't think so. He told me that Conrad was only awful to me because that's how I behaved to him."

"He had a chance to change. Professor Tooth brought him here to give him a second chance. And what did he do with it? He threatened to hurt Delaney and he tried to sell us all to save himself."

"I know." She paused and tucked her feet in as a wave crept up to wash away part of her sand drawing. "I just want to talk to Paris again." She tossed her stick into the tide. "He made friends with Conrad. He's going to feel bad that Conrad's gone."

"Yeah, that's true. But things happen for a reason."

"Brodie..." Darrell's voice dropped to a whisper, and he ducked his head to hear. "I can't remember all of it." She looked at his face, serious and kind. *He looks so old. Not like a kid at all, anymore.*

"What *do* you remember?" he asked. "Do you remember the fire?"

She nodded. "Yeah — both of them. I remember waking up on the floor of the lighthouse and feeling hot. I remember pulling Kate to her feet and grabbing your arm."

"The smoke was so thick by then, I could hardly see." Brodie reached down to Delaney. "I followed you out, dog." He looked at Darrell again. "Do you remember the coast guard boat?"

"Spraying water at the lighthouse?"

"Yeah. It was too late by the time they got here, though. All they could do was contain the fire. Not that there was anything else out here that would burn. The new beacon is solid concrete."

"Brodie — do you think we brought the fire with us somehow?"

He chuckled. "No. The word is that the fire department is still investigating, but they think that someone shot a flare off inside the lighthouse and some of the old rags and debris inside ignited."

Darrell looked horrified. "What if they find out it was us?"

"They're not going to find out. We were back at school almost a full hour before the fire department made it out here. They have no idea we were even there. And that lighthouse was so old, it was like a giant candle waiting to burn."

"But what about the flare gun?"

Brodie grinned. "Boris Meirz was talking to one of the firefighters and they told him they had found an old flare gun. It was pretty charred, but I'm sure they'll find it registered to Conrad's dad." He picked up a rock and tossed it into the surf. "Boris said they think it belonged to a poacher or a smuggler who had been using the lighthouse as a place to hide. It'll just confirm their theory if it turns out to be registered to Conrad's father."

"And what if it's not? I can't imagine Conrad's dad doing something as legal as registering a flare gun."

Brodie looked out over the water. "It doesn't matter who the gun is registered to, Darrell. The only person who touched it was Conrad, and there is no evidence we were anywhere near the lighthouse." He paused. "Kate's going to be okay, y'know. I just looked in on her in your room."

Darrell nodded, but even though her friends were safe, she felt a lump the size of a boulder bloom in her throat. She had always hated and feared Conrad, but now he was lost forever and it was her fault. She felt like crying tears enough to fill the ocean lapping at her feet.

"Is he just gone — as if he'd never been here? Is he lost forever?"

"Darrell — there's nothing you can do. It's over."

She felt tiredness wash through her again like a wave and stood up, almost staggering.

"You'd better take your girl to get some sleep, Delaney," Brodie said, patting the dog as he got to his feet. They walked back to the path, Darrell leaning heavily on Brodie's arm for support.

"Leg still a bit sore?"

"Yeah, but it's not too bad. My prosthesis feels wonderful after the wooden piano leg." Delaney ran ahead on the beach, sniffing. "You know, it's funny how things happen," she said as they turned onto the path to the school.

"What do you mean?"

"Well, the Renaissance was supposed to be a time of light — a time when mankind awoke from the darkness of ignorance and poverty."

Brodie looked surprised. "Well, what I saw of it was amazing. Look at the work done by Leonardo — and the awesome cathedral. Pretty different from the bleak times we saw during the Black Plague."

"I know. It's — well, there were a lot of black shadows during the Renaissance, too. All the weapons Leonardo had to design, and the wars that never stopped being fought."

"I guess so. It was an incredible era."

"Yeah." She sighed. "It's too bad we saw only such a little bit of it."

Brodie laughed as they walked into the back garden of the school and past the old arbutus tree. "Well, this *is* Eagle Glen, Darrell. You never know what is going to happen next. Maybe you will get to see more of Leonardo and his time."

She shook her head and sighed. "I doubt that. Let's talk about something else. What are you planning for Christmastime?"

"My dad has rented us a house near Drumheller for the holidays," Brodie said, as they walked up the front steps of the school. "I think I'll go see if I can find me a dino bone or two at the Tyrell Museum."

"Knowing you, it'll be a whole T. Rex," Darrell tried to smile, but couldn't quite manage it. "My mom is going back to Europe over Christmas with Doctors Without Borders," she said. "She has fewer meetings this time, so she said I could go with her to sketch some of the sights."

Brodie chuckled. "Any place in particular?" he asked.

"Well, she *is* going to Italy," Darrell said, "but she

also said something about sunny Spain. It might be nice to get out of the rain for awhile."

"Send me a postcard, okay?"

She nodded and waved goodbye to Brodie before turning to drag herself up the stairs behind Delaney. Lily had gone home already, and Kate's bed was tousled but empty, so she sat alone in her room and began to remove her prosthesis. She felt like falling back into her marshmallow pillows and sleeping for days, but before she could lie down she heard a quiet knock.

"May I come in?"

Darrell nodded. "Would you like to sit down?"

Professor Myrtle Tooth waved Darrell back to her bed and pulled Kate's chair out from beside her desk.

Darrell sat down on the bed, left leg tucked underneath her, and waited for Professor Tooth to speak.

"I suspect you may already know what I am going to say." Professor Tooth looked at Darrell, her voice calm. "Conrad Kennedy is missing. He appears to have run away from school."

Darrell nodded again. "Mrs. Follett told me he had been sent to another school."

"I'm afraid Mrs. Follett was misled. The telephone call she received during my absence was not from another school. The police are trying to trace the number, but as it appears to have originated from a stolen cellular telephone, I suspect they will not have much luck."

Despair swept through Darrell and threatened to swallow her whole. She dropped her face into her hands and thought of the shattered lighthouse, reduced to rubble on the shore.

"I have a question for you Darrell, and I would appreciate it if you would look at me."

She lifted her head from her hands and looked at Professor Tooth, into eyes clear and green as bottomless pools.

"Do you know where Conrad is right now?"

She couldn't believe it. The principal had asked her the one question to which she could reply with complete honesty.

"I'm sorry, Professor Tooth. I have no idea," Darrell answered.

And that was that.

Professor Tooth stood up. At the door she turned. "A very clever man I once met told me something interesting a long time ago. Now, how did he put it? 'One cannot turn back when one is bound to a star.' Or words to that effect, I believe."

Darrell gaped, unable to speak.

"You have now spent your first full term at Eagle Glen, Darrell. Look to the stars, my dear. I'm afraid that, for you, there is no turning back."

The last rays of the setting sun shone in through the large, curving window.

"Winter solstice," Myrtle Tooth said quietly. "The days will grow longer again beginning tomorrow. Perhaps it may interest you," she remarked thoughtfully, "to hear of the special class I have in mind for the new term. Reformation and Inquisition, I believe I'll call it."

Darrell swallowed. "It sounds — interesting, Professor Tooth."

"I hope so," she said. "It will not be for the faint of heart, but I do believe it will be well suited for those — seasoned — travellers who like to take a very close look at that which has come before."

She closed the door quietly and was gone.

Darrell pulled the notebook from the table beside her bed and spent a few quiet moments tracing her finger along the first words she had copied from Leonardo's notes.

He turns not back who is bound to a star.

The door opened again and she looked up, not sure which of the million or so questions she should ask first. But instead of Professor Tooth, Kate stood in the doorway, looking tired but grinning a crooked little smile.

"I've just had the weirdest conversation with Professor Tooth," she said, as she sat on Darrell's bed.

"Me too," replied Darrell, not having a clue where to begin. "Are you okay, Katie?"

"Yep." Kate nodded and her hair blazed in the light of the setting sun. "I think it's safe to say we have an interesting term ahead of us. Oh — and Professor Tooth asked me to give you this. She said she thought you might need a new one." She flipped a clean notebook into her friend's lap.

For the first time in that very long day, Darrell found herself able to smile.